# THE WITCH'S LOST SPELL

## WITCHES OF BEFANA BAY, BOOK 3

## DEANNA CHASE

# ABOUT THIS BOOK

Indigo Easton, owner of Brooms that Vroom, is a witch with secrets. There are reasons why she rarely dates and has decided marriage and a traditional family isn't for her. But when the sexy Niko Morales, a fling from a past vacation, walks into her town and is determined to make her his, she's not sure she can resist him. Just as she's letting her guard down, a dangerous spell from her past is cast on a young college student and everyone starts pointing fingers at Indigo. Now she has to prove her innocence and somehow keep her secrets hidden or she risks losing everything, including the man who just might be the love of her life.

Niko Morales, an agent with the Magical Task Force, has always been a bit of an outsider. With the last of his family gone, he's settled in Befana Bay near his two best friends and the woman that he's never forgotten. After just one weekend together, Niko knew Indigo Easton was the one for him and is determined to win her heart. But when he's assigned to a cold case that points to her as the main suspect, he has no choice but to prove her innocence because there's no way he's going to be the one to take down the only woman he's ever loved.

# CHAPTER 1

"THIS IS A MISTAKE," Indigo said as she stared at herself in the full-length mirror. Her dark hair was pulled up into a wavy ponytail, showing off her long neck. The sapphire blue wraparound blouse hugged her in all the right place, and her jeans were doing fabulous things for her backside.

"That color of blue is never a mistake," her younger sister Lily said, giving her a look of approval. "If I showed up on a date looking like that, I think Brax would probably drag me off to the nearest coat closet."

"He'd drag you off no matter what you were wearing," Indigo said, rolling her eyes. Lily and Braxton were still in the honeymoon phase of their relationship. Keeping their hands to themselves definitely wasn't in the cards. "Besides, I wasn't talking about this." She waved a hand at her outfit. "I mean the date. I shouldn't be going out with Niko at all. He's an investigator for the Magical Task Force of all things!"

Lily brushed her blond hair out of her sparkling blue eyes and stared impatiently at her sister. "Niko isn't Paul."

"Of course he isn't," Indigo said. "But that doesn't mean I can trust him. What do you think will happen when he finds out about my past? Even if he believed me, I'd be detrimental to his career if anyone ever dug that up."

"Indy," Lily said softly as she moved to stand next to her sister. "Brax says that Niko is the most loyal person he knows. Don't you think it's unfair to judge him before you even give him a chance? He was relentless in bringing down Brax's ex, you know."

"Yeah, I know. But that doesn't change things for me and you know why," Indigo said. Braxton and Niko grew up together and were best friends. Of course Brax thought he was loyal. And he was definitely grateful after Niko had helped save Lily from being tortured by Brax's power-obsessed nightmare of an ex-girlfriend who had cursed him all those years ago. But Indigo barely knew Niko. They'd spent one night together over a year ago. A mind-blowing, unforgettable night. But still, that was before she knew he was an agent for the Magical Task Force.

The buzzer sounded, indicating that someone was at the door.

"Too late. You can't send him away now." Lily practically flew to the door to greet Niko.

Indigo took a deep breath, smoothed her hair one more time, and then strode out into the living room. While the one-bedroom apartment that was above her store, Brooms that Vroom, wasn't terribly large, it did make for a convenient commute. Her office was next door and the shop just downstairs.

"Niko, don't you look handsome," Lily said as she waved Indigo's date inside. "Is that jacket new?" Lily eyed him with appreciation as she ran her hand down his leather-clad arm.

Indigo narrowed her eyes at her sister as a tiny ball of jealousy hit her out of nowhere. *Stop it*, she ordered herself. Lily had no interest in Niko. She was happily loved up with Braxton. Besides, Indigo couldn't make a claim on the man she had zero intention of dating. Tonight was just a one-off thing.

"It is." Niko smirked at her. "Now stop flirting with me before your sister gets violent."

"Violent?" Indigo scoffed as she shook her head at him, hating that he saw right through her. "You flatter yourself."

Lily chuckled and stared pointedly at Indigo's fists. When she met her sister's gaze, she lifted one eyebrow.

Indigo walked over to the door and held it open. "Tell Brax hello for me."

Lily took the hint, and while shaking her head, she strode out the door. But then she paused and looked back. "Have a good night, you two."

"I plan on it," Niko said. He had his hands stuffed in the front of his jeans pockets and was rocking on his heels.

"That's the last time I invite you over," Indigo muttered to Lily before shutting the door on her sister. Lily's laughter could be heard for the next few seconds as she descended the stairs.

"By the time this date is over, you won't even remember you said that." Niko winked at her. "Ready to get dinner?"

"As ready as I'm ever gonna be," she said, sounding more annoyed than she'd intended. It wasn't Niko's fault that she was determined not to date him. Or that what she really wanted to do was forget dinner and tug him into the bedroom. If she had her way, she'd recreate the night they'd spent together in Florida and then cease any further contact with him.

Would that even work? Now that Niko had moved to Washington permanently, he'd been a constant presence in her hometown. Of course he was. When he wasn't working or at his own house in the neighboring city of Hansville, he was spending time with his two best friends, Brax and Dante. Keeping her distance from him was going to be nearly impossible. Especially if he kept showing up at Brooms that Vroom to rent a magical broom every week when he went on rides during the sunrise instead of just buying one like a normal witch.

"How do you feel about Italian?" Niko asked as he opened the passenger door of his shiny new blue Dodge Ram truck.

"Are you kidding?" Indigo asked, her expression incredulous. "You do realize my grandmother's surname is Befana, right? Old world Italian. Deep roots. It doesn't get deeper than that."

Niko snorted. "Yeah, I knew that. So it's a yes?"

"As long as it's really *good* Italian." Indigo climbed into the truck. Once he joined her, she eyed him suspiciously. "Are we going somewhere outside of Befana Bay? Because ever since Ricci's closed, we haven't had any decent Italian other than Enzo's Pizza."

"No. Not leaving Befana Bay," he said as he put the truck in gear and headed down Main Street. "And we're not going to Enzo's."

"You're not going to tell me?" she asked, suddenly amused. She'd always been attracted to men with a bit of mystery.

"Nope. It's a surprise."

Indigo couldn't help the small smile that claimed her lips. "This should be interesting."

He glanced over at her and winked before turning his attention back to the road. They drove out of the downtown area and out onto the two-lane highway.

"I thought we weren't leaving Befana Bay," Indigo said, her eyebrows raised.

"We're not." He slowed and took a sharp right turn onto Befana Meadow Road and then pulled into a small parking lot. He killed the engine and smiled over at her.

Indigo looked up at the Gothic-looking library and then back at him. The library had closed about ten years ago when the state budget had been cut. She'd known the building was for sale but hadn't heard of anyone purchasing it. From the looks of things, both the parking lot and the building had been cleaned up recently. In fact, the building looked better than ever. It had been freshly painted, and the landscaping was tidy with abundant flowers lining the pathway to the front door.

Niko jumped out of the truck, and a moment later he opened her door and held out a hand to help her down.

"Care to explain?" she asked as the pair walked up to the front door.

"Sure, but let's get inside first."

The moment they started up the steps, the lanterns lining the stairs lit, casting a pleasant glow. Vines of fragrant orange honeysuckle materialized out of thin air, covering the handrails, and the front door slowly opened as chimes welcomed them into the gorgeous building.

Indigo glanced up at Niko, her eyes wide with surprise. "Did you have anything to do with this?"

He shrugged one shoulder as he gave her a cheeky smile.

Indigo stared, utterly amazed as they stepped into the candlelit library. They walked through the marble entry and into the main section of the library. The floor-to-ceiling shelves were stuffed solid with books, and there was a table set for two right in the middle of the room.

Niko held a chair out for her and then took his seat across from her. "I thought a quiet, private dinner might be nice before we head out on that moonlit kayak trip."

"What... How..." Indigo shook her head, unable to process what he'd planned. Then she leaned forward as she held his gorgeous gaze. "Is this building haunted or something? Housing werewolves? Or vampires?"

"What?" he asked with a laugh. "No, why would you ask that?"

Indigo shrugged just as a server dressed in all black arrived and filled their water glasses from a carafe. "I figured the Magical Task Force must have purchased this building. Why else would you have access to it?"

"You think the MTF imprisons vampires?" he asked, his eyes glinting with humor.

"Yes. I'm certain they deal with every magical creature."

Indigo sat up straight, her shoulders back, suddenly very interested in everything he had to say. "They do, don't they? Are they in the basement? Will I get a tour later?"

Niko let out a bark of laughter. "We can take a tour of the basement after dinner, but I fear all you'll find is boxes of inventory."

"Inventory? Of what, magical handcuffs?" she asked before she could think that through.

"Now that *would* be interesting," he said with a smirk.

Indigo felt her face flush with heat but willed herself to keep eye contact as she rose to the challenge. "It would, wouldn't it?"

"There's a reason why I never forgot you." He reached across the table and covered her hand with his, squeezing gently.

Indigo stared down at the connection for a few beats and then slowly pulled her hand away. The spark between them was entirely too intimate. Too comfortable. Too... everything. She should have never agreed to this date. After letting out a long breath, she raised her gaze and focused on the books surrounding them. "Tell me about the library. How did you manage all this?" She waved her hand at their surroundings. "And why does it look like this place never closed down ten years ago?"

"Dante purchased it and turned it into a bookstore," he said nonchalantly as if he hadn't just dropped massive news out of nowhere. "Remember when I said I'd take you to dinner and a bookstore? I figured this would be a little more special than taking you places you've already been."

Indigo stared at him, speechless for a long moment.

Then she blinked and shook her head. Dante was Niko and Brax's best friend. He'd moved to Befana Bay about six months ago and as far as Indigo knew, he was working at Brax's outdoor shop just down the street from her broom shop. "Dante bought the building and turned it into a bookstore? Why did I not know about this?"

"He's been keeping it close to the vest, making sure the sale went through before he told anyone."

"But it's all fixed up and there are books everywhere," Indigo said. "The sale didn't just close last week."

"True. I'm sure Dante has his reasons. He's announcing it tomorrow, so he said it was okay to show you tonight. Lily learned about it yesterday but was kind enough to keep it a surprise." He nodded to someone over her shoulder.

A handsome server with dark hair and startling blue eyes arrived, someone Indigo didn't recognize, and filled their water glasses. He then snapped his fingers, summoning two wine glasses that landed with a soft thump onto the table. "Red or white?" he asked.

"Red," they both said at the same time.

The server reached for a bottle perched on a side table that Indigo hadn't noticed when they'd arrived and proceeded to pour their wine. When he was done, he wiped the bottle with a cloth napkin and said, "Your first course will be out in just a moment."

"Thank you, Mateo, I appreciate you helping me out tonight," Niko said.

"Of course, Mr. Morales." Mateo gave him a slight bow before he retreated.

Niko rolled his eyes at the man and shook his head, looking amused.

"Friend of yours?" Indigo asked.

"You could say that. He's Dante's store manager. He's also the one responsible for the landscaping and renovations around here."

"That's... wow." Indigo glanced around, looking for the striking man. "I've never met him before. He's new around here, isn't he?"

Niko let out a bark of laughter. "Yep. But Dante's known him forever. He's his stepbrother. But enough about Mateo. How do you feel about lobster ravioli in an asiago cream sauce?"

Indigo felt a smile claim her lips as she beamed at him. There was no way he'd guessed her favorite meal all on his own. "You've been talking to my sisters, haven't you?"

"I do my homework." He winked at her, and Mateo placed the antipasto course in front of them.

"You know what, Niko Morales?" she said, taking a sip of her wine.

"What's that, Indigo Easton?"

"You're a really good date."

# CHAPTER 2

NIKO WATCHED as Indigo drained the last of her wine. She was lovely, her cheeks rosy and her eyes sparkling with pleasure. He'd had a stroke of genius when he'd questioned Lily about Indigo's favorite meal. His grandmother had taught him how to cook when he was just a boy, and while he didn't do it often, it was something he was proud of.

"I can't believe you made this yourself," Indigo said as she placed her elbows on the table and leaned forward once the plates were removed. "You're just full of surprises."

"Lucky for you, I'm not quite done." He stood and held his hand out to her.

Indigo slipped her warm hand into his as she rose from the table. "I can't wait to see what you have up your sleeve this time."

Warmth filled Niko's chest as he led her over to the bookcases. The moment they neared, books in two distinctive sections started to glow.

Indigo reached her fingertips toward the glowing spines, but just before she touched one, she snatched her hand back and turned to Niko, her brow pinched. "What's this?"

"The store and books have been spelled to pick up on each customer's interests. The books they are most interested in will glow to help them find what they want. You can also just ask for something, and those will light up too."

Indigo blinked. "Really? You're telling me that if I pull one of these books, it's going to be something I want to read?"

Niko gave her a half shrug. "That's the theory. Why don't you try it and let me know how it worked?"

"All right. Let's see." Indigo narrowed her eyes as she scanned the glowing spines. "It would be better if I could actually see the titles of the books."

"Dante thought about that, but he likes the idea of each book being a surprise," Niko said.

"Hmm, okay." She reached for one of the books and pulled it out. One look at the cover and her expression changed from slight skepticism to pure delight. "Oh my gosh. I've been wanting to read this one."

She held up a book with a bright purple cover that read *Alpacas and Alibis* on the cover. "It's a cozy mystery series that's been on my radar, but I haven't been able to get to it yet."

"I guess the spell works," Niko said, feeling a little smug, considering he was the one that cast the spell for Dante.

Indigo turned her attention back to the books, eagerly going through the lit-up spines. She had a nice pile when she finally pulled one that wasn't lit with magic. After a moment, she pushed it back onto the shelf. "This one is a little too procedural for me."

Niko glanced at her pile. "Did you find any new authors, or were all of them writers you've read before?" It was something he'd worried about when he cast the spell.

"Oh, no. There are new authors here. I'm impressed, Niko. Please tell Dante for me."

He smiled. "Happy to." Then he nodded to the lit-up section that was behind her. "What about those? You haven't even gotten to them yet."

"Oh, my. I'm going to go broke if I look at any more books," she said even as she moved to inspect the next batch.

"The books are on me," Niko said. "Get whatever you want." He had been the one to invite her out, after all. Plus, considering he was a silent partner who'd invested in the store, he wasn't interested in taking her money.

"No way! This pile is going to cost a mint. I can't let you do that."

"You can," he assured her. "In fact, I insist. If I'd taken you to dinner, it would've cost more."

"It's not about that, It's..." She trailed off as she shook her head. "I'm not letting you buy my books."

"All right. If that's what you want." He held his hands up, knowing that the point-of-sale system wouldn't be installed until the next day, and currently there was no way to ring her up.

"It is." Indigo turned from him to inspect the second shelf of glowing books. She pulled one out and visibly recoiled before quickly replacing the book back onto the shelf. "I think I have plenty to keep me busy," she said as she turned away from the shelf and looked at him. "Ready to go?"

Niko blinked at her, slightly taken aback. "Did the spell get it wrong? If those books—"

"No, it was fine. I promise," she said, her cheeks turning a deep shade of pink. "I just think this is plenty for now."

"You're sure? Cause it kinda looked like maybe the spell got it wrong," he said, wanting to make sure the spell wasn't going to turn anyone off.

"I'm sure." She pasted a bright smile on her face. "I'm just ready for that moonlit kayak ride you promised me."

"Absolutely." Niko glanced back at the shelf, still feeling as if he was missing something. She hadn't liked what she saw, but it was clear she didn't want to talk about it. He'd have to make a note to have a few more people test out the spell. "Right this way, gorgeous."

"Wait." She pulled a few bills out of her bag and placed them on the table. "For the books. And don't bother to try and refuse it. You aren't winning this one."

Niko chuckled softly, knowing when he was outmatched. "You're a tough negotiator." He held his arm out to her. "It only makes me like you more. I love a strong woman."

Indigo rolled her eyes but slipped her arm through his and fell into step beside him as they left the old library.

Niko stared at Indigo's wonderous expression and knew he was a goner. He'd known she was special ever since the night they'd spent together back in Florida. The moment she'd left his hotel room, he'd kicked himself for not pushing harder to get her contact information. He'd asked, but she'd been coy and said something about having just one magical night. And since he'd known that she was on vacation, how could he argue with that?

But now, they lived less than twenty miles from each other. For some reason, she was reluctant to date someone in law enforcement. He could only guess at what she'd experienced in the past. He'd heard stories of abusive agents and had even been involved in testifying against another officer after he'd witnessed a disturbing incident involving the agent's wife. So he understood. He just wished she'd give him a chance to show that he was safe.

"Stop staring at me like that," Indigo said from her kayak. They'd stopped paddling and were just floating in a cove. One that was a known playground for a pod of orcas. With any luck, they'd show up and make this night even more special.

"Like what?" He gave her a half smile, openly admiring her pale features that were illuminated by the moonlight.

"Like you can't wait to peel my clothes off and have me for dessert," she said dryly.

Niko let his gaze travel down her torso while he made zero effort to hide his desire. It was true. He did want to take her home and strip all her clothing away. A sudden image of them in the shower together flashed in his mind. What he wouldn't give to have his hands on her soapy body.

"Niko!" she said in a loud whisper. "Stop. My clothes are going to spontaneously combust if you keep that up."

He couldn't help the self-satisfied chuckled that escaped his lips. It was so gratifying to know that he wasn't the only one who was affected by the chemistry sparking between them.

She shook her head, but he didn't miss the shy smile that she tried to hide.

Just as he was about to tease her about wanting him, she sucked in a sharp gasp. "Niko, look!"

He followed her pointed gaze and felt a wave of calm wash over him. A large dorsal fin was gliding through the water straight toward them. The large female orca emerged from the water, showing her head and body before she dove back down under the surface. The minute she submerged, a smaller orca with a peach tint to the white parts of its body mimicked her motion.

"Arabella trusts us," Indigo said, her tone hushed with awe. "She's brought her baby to meet us."

"How old do you think the baby is?" Niko asked her, knowing he was experiencing something extraordinary. The witches of Befana Bay had a special relationship with the resident orcas. Often, they showed up during the paddleboard coven meetings that were held at dawn, and if he remembered correctly, August West, Sage Easton's significant other, could talk to the magnificent beasts.

"It can't be more than a week," Indigo said, her eyes misting with tears of joy. "I saw Arabella the last time I was out kayaking and there was no baby with her then. And if anyone had seen a baby, it would be big news. Baby orcas have a tough survival rate here in the Salish Sea. We'll need to do everything we can to help Arabella with her little one."

"How do we help?" he asked.

"The witches will do a protection spell and call on the goddesses for an abundance of Chinook salmon for them to feed on." She wiped the lone tear that had rolled down her cheek. "Arabella lost a baby four years ago. It was tragic. Everyone will be on full alert with this new little one."

Niko was silent as he watched the large mother sluice through the water with her offspring beside her. There was such a wonderous joy that radiated from the pair. He prayed to the goddess that the new baby was strong and continued to thrive.

When Arabella and her calf finally slipped away into the night, Indigo paddled over so that she was right next to Niko. Placing her oar over her lap, she leaned over and gave him a whisper of a kiss on his cheek. "Thank you, Niko. I think this might be the best date I've ever had."

He wanted to reach for her. To take her hand in his and tug her close again, kiss her under the moonlight, but she already had her paddle in the water and was headed back toward shore.

Twenty minutes later, Niko walked Indigo up the stairs to her apartment above her broom shop. Once she had her key in her hand, she turned to him. "Well, I guess this is goodnight."

"Same time next week?" he asked, brushing a lock of dark hair that had escaped her ponytail out of her eyes.

She took a step back as her eyebrows shot up. "Same time next week for what? Dinner and a kayak ride?"

"Sure. Or we can do something else if you prefer. Movie. Dancing. Midnight rollerblading. Or my personal favorite, drinks on the porch swing while we watch the moonrise."

Indigo's smile faded as regret flashed in her eyes. With a frown, she stepped forward and placed her palm against his cheek. "You have no idea how much I'd like that, but it wouldn't be fair to you. I don't date law enforcement."

He'd been expecting the rejection, but he wasn't going down without a fight. "What if we just never talk about my job? Just think of me as the eccentric bookstore investor who is a little mysterious. Women like that, right?"

"You invested in Dante's bookstore?" she asked, surprise making her cheeks flush.

"I'm a silent partner," he said with a shrug. "I've always loved bookstores, and I can't think of anyone else I'd rather be in business with than him. Brax would be okay, too, but he wasn't looking for investors."

She sucked in a breath and slowly let it out. "If you were just an eccentric bookstore investor, I'd likely be inviting you in right now, but you deserve someone who will be all in with you, and that's not me." Indigo leaned in and brushed a light kiss across his lips before turning and disappearing into her apartment.

Niko stood on her porch for a long moment, feeling a pang of disappointment in his gut. He had no idea who had made her distrust those in law enforcement, but if he had his way, he'd hunt them down and make them pay for whatever wrongs they'd inflicted on her.

With his head bowed, he descended her steps, knowing she was always going to be the one who got away.

# CHAPTER 3

THE SUN SHONE through the front window of her apartment, and even though it was a bright, sunny day, Indigo felt as if a cloud was hovering over her head. She'd woken up that morning with a heaviness on her heart. She couldn't shake the feeling that she'd lost something—or someone—that was very special.

Grabbing her insulated coffee mug, she went next door to her office and took a seat at her desk, intending to process invoices for the month. Instead, she found herself staring at the safe beneath her desk and thinking about the notebooks she'd stashed there the day she'd taken over the broom shop from her grandmother. Bethany had stepped in to run it temporarily after her son and daughter-in-law died in case one of her granddaughters decided they wanted to take it over.

The store had been in the Befana family ever since the town had been founded over two centuries ago. Though in the early days it was more of an apothecary that carried other magical supplies. And although Indigo still carried some herbs and charms, she'd morphed the main business into magical brooms. And with it, she'd changed the name from Befana Bay's Witchery and Brooms to the snappier name, Brooms that Vroom.

No one in her family had questioned why she'd made the changes. They knew.

Indigo tore her gaze away from the safe that held the answers to those questions and reminded herself that since she'd locked away her secrets, she'd built a good life. A happy life. One that she could be proud of.

And welcoming a man who worked for the Magical Task Force into that life was just asking for trouble she didn't need.

The store phone rang, startling Indigo out of her memories. She picked up the cordless and said, "Brooms that Vroom, Indigo speaking. How can I help you?"

After taking a reservation for rentals for a family of four that weekend, Indigo quickly got the invoices paid and then went down to open the shop.

As she was moving a display of broom rentals onto the sidewalk in front of the store, a young woman with sleek brown hair and wide amber eyes walked up.

"Hello, are you Indigo?" the woman asked.

"In the flesh," Indigo said with a welcoming smile. "Are you in the market for a broom?"

"Not exactly." She pulled a thick piece of paper from a book bag she had slung around her body and held it out.

"I'm here about the job you have advertised in the *Befana Bay Bulletin*. I hope the position is still open."

Indigo nodded as she took the woman's résumé. She scanned it, noting that the woman was short on experience but that she was a student at a local magical college who was majoring in business administration and minoring in graphic design. Indigo's interest piqued. She'd been wanting to run some online and print campaigns and needed a decent graphic designer. She glanced at her name at the top and then said, "It's nice to meet you, Kinsley. The position is still open. Why don't you come on in and we'll chat a bit."

"I'd love to." Kinsley followed Indigo into the store and then paused for a moment to look around at all the brooms. "My gosh. Look at those carved handles. I've never seen such beautiful, intricate work before."

"They're lovely, aren't they?" Indigo agreed, nodding at the carved handles that depicted secret gardens that had lifelike flowers inlaid in the wood. "Those are carved in Italy by a master craftsman and imported. The ones on the opposite wall are done by a local craftsman. While not quite as intricate, I find the subtle landscape designs fascinating. And just look at the hidden animals peeking out everywhere."

"Oh my." Kinsley pressed a hand to her heart as she inspected the broom handles thoroughly. "Maybe I should change my major to art. How lovely it must be to be able to work on these all day."

Indigo chuckled. "I'm certain a business degree will serve you well. If you do decide to pursue art as a living, having the tools to figure out how to sell it will be invaluable."

Kinsley let out a sigh and smiled softly. "You sound like my mother."

"Oh, oops." Indigo grinned at her. "I guess I've turned that corner from dreamer to responsible adult." She faked a shudder and added, "It's probably all downhill from here."

Giggling, Kinsley shook her head. "Looks like you have years until things start to deteriorate."

"Now you're just flattering me. Thank you." Chuckling, Indigo leaned against the checkout counter and said, "Tell me about yourself and why you want to work here."

"Oh, I'm starting my senior year at the Witchery Institute in the fall, and my plan once I'm done with school is to open a store much like this with my sister. Only I'll be specializing in tarot cards and talismans while she focuses on herbs and potions. Mostly healing and spiritual stuff. I wanted to get experience working in a store that caters to the witch community. I did work for a psychic during the school year, booking her appointments and doing her advertising, but none of that involved retail. She moved to Salem to be near family a few months ago, so I've been looking for something that will give me more experience in the direction I'm wanting to go."

Indigo studied the young woman, trying to get a read on her energy. She wasn't an empath, but she had learned over the years that if she was quiet enough, she could usually get a good understanding of someone's overall intentions.

There was nothing but love and light coming from the woman standing in front of her. It made her inclined to offer her the job on the spot, but there were more questions she had to ask first.

"You said you'll be focusing on tarot. Are you a reader?" Indigo asked.

"Yes." An easy smile claimed Kinsley's lips as her eyes lit up. "It's something that runs in my family. All the oldest women in each generation are gifted with the sight when it comes to tarot. I do readings as well as design the cards. It's pretty much my passion. If you want me to offer readings here, I'm more than happy to."

It was an interesting idea, but Indigo didn't think tarot readings really went that well with her brand. "Maybe save those for festivals or special events."

"That works, too." Kinsley was clearly ready to say yes to anything in order to get a shot at working at the store.

Her eagerness charmed Indigo. She'd been fresh-faced and eager to learn anything and everything about her passions at one time, too. So eager that it had almost ruined her life. She quickly pushed those memories aside and focused on the woman in front of her. "The job is part-time, but the pay is competitive. We need someone for Fridays, Saturdays, and Sundays. And sometimes Mondays. Will that be an issue?"

"Not at all. I'm available whenever you need me," she said. "And then when I go back to school, if you still need weekend help, I'm your gal."

Indigo asked her a few more questions, and by the time the door chimed, indicating they had a customer, Kinsley had already filled out her new hire paperwork.

"Good morning," a familiar deep voice said.

Jerking her head up, Indigo sucked in a sharp breath when she spotted Niko heading toward her. He had an easy smile, and his T-shirt was molded to his sculpted chest. The man was far too gorgeous for his own good.

His lips curved into a cocky smile.

She rolled her eyes and turned to tell Kinsley that she could start in the morning, but before she could get the words out, the younger woman was already striding toward Niko.

"Hello," Kinsley said, far too eagerly. When she reached him, she placed her hand on his forearm and stared up at him adoringly. "What can I help you with this morning?"

Amusement lit his dark eyes as he smiled down at her and then cast his gaze to Indigo. "New employee?"

Indigo nodded as she reached for Niko's favorite broom. Holding it in her hands, she said, "Niko, meet Kinsley. Kinsley, this is Niko. He's been renting the same broom each week for almost a month now."

"You've been renting a broom every week? Wouldn't it be more cost effective to just buy one?" Kinsley asked, looking confused.

"Yes, it would," Indigo answered for him. "After the cost of the third rental, he'd have been ahead if he'd just bought the same broom. I've been trying to tell him that."

He shrugged. "If I did that, I wouldn't have an excuse to come in here all the time."

Kinsley glanced between Niko and Indigo, realization dawning in her amber eyes. "I see. Maybe I should just get out from under foot then." She raised her eyebrows at Indigo. "What time tomorrow?"

"Nine sharp," Indigo said, briefly tearing her gaze from Niko.

"I'll be here."

Indigo didn't miss the way Kinsley checked out Niko's backside on her way out, and she couldn't help her grunt of disapproval.

Niko chuckled softly.

"What?" Indigo asked defensively.

"I just find it amusing that you're jealous. That's all."

"I'm not jealous," she lied.

"If you say so." He winked at her and handed over his credit card.

Without a word, Indigo completed the transaction for his broom rental. As he was signing, he said, "Are you sure I can't entice you to join me on a moonlit broom ride tonight? I heard there's a chance that we'll see the northern lights."

His invitation was tempting. So tempting that she almost said yes, but before she could get the word out, she remembered the promise she'd made herself the night before not to accept any more dates from him, no matter how charming he was when he asked her out. She quickly clamped her mouth closed and then shook her head.

"Are you sure? I was planning to grab a beer and a burger at the Salt Circle before my ride. I'd love to have some company."

"Niko," Indigo started before she let out an audible sigh. "We're not dating."

"Can't we be friends?" he asked as he frowned at her.

"Of course we can. It's just…" *Dammit.*

"It's just what?" he asked, frowning.

She swallowed the lump in her throat and decided it was best to be honest. "I think we both know that we'll never be just friends. Having dinner or going on a broom ride with you will just make it harder to walk away." Indigo's stomach churned as she spotted her new employee outside on the sidewalk with a phone pressed to her ear. In an effort to break the cycle of Niko always asking her out, she hastily added, "Maybe you should invite Kinsley. I bet she'd love to do both."

Irritation flashed in his gaze before he said, "Yeah, maybe I will."

Indigo watched him walk out the front door and stop to talk to the gorgeous college student. Bile rose in the back of her throat as she watched Kinsley gaze up at him with adoration.

Unable to watch any more, Indigo turned her back on them and then started reorganizing the brooms, just so she'd have something to do.

# CHAPTER 4

THE FRUSTRATION CURLING in Niko's gut had him striding out the door of Indigo's shop. The knowledge that Indigo wanted to date him but wouldn't, for whatever reason, was driving him insane. He couldn't stop the ache he had for her, but he also knew there wasn't anything to do but walk away. She'd made herself clear, and as much as he hated it, he intended to respect that.

"Oh, hello again," Kinsley said, gazing up at him with a warm smile.

"Hi," he said, forcing a smile for the younger woman.

She glanced at his broom. "Are you headed out for a ride now?"

He shook his head. "I'll go later. Probably at twilight. It's a nice way to unwind at the end of the day." Really, he'd likely just go home, prop the broom up against his wall, and then head out to his studio to try to get lost in woodworking. He needed something to take his mind off Indigo, and flying around on one of her brooms wasn't going to be the distraction he needed.

She placed her hand on his arm and leaned in. "That sounds lovely. Do you mind if I join you?"

Caught off guard, Niko blinked once and then said, "Sure. Why not?" Then immediately he glanced back at Indigo's shop. It was what she'd suggested. Maybe this was just the thing he needed to put the idea of dating Indigo behind him. "We could meet down at the marina at 6:30."

"That sounds good." Kinsley glowed with happiness. But then her phone buzzed with a text, and she frowned as she read the message. "Oh no. Now what am I going to do?" She looked up and glanced around, her expression worried.

"What's wrong?" Niko asked, ready to go into problem-solving mode. "What can I do to help?"

"Oh, you're sweet," she said, relief washing over her face. "I just need a ride home. My sister borrowed my car today, and she's stuck in Seattle for a few more hours. I suppose I can call a cab. Are there any that run in Befana Bay?"

"Probably, but they'll need to come from Poulsbo, and it'll cost you," he said, already pulling his keys out of his pocket. No one could ever accuse him of not being a gentleman. "Don't worry about that. I've got you. Come on."

"Oh my gosh! You're the best." Kinsley grabbed his arm and pressed her head against his biceps. "I can't thank you enough."

"No thanks necessary."

Kinsley eagerly tightened her grip on him as he led her down the street to his truck.

IF THERE WAS a way to cast a spell to time travel, Niko would have already pulled that trigger. He should have canceled his broom ride date with Kinsley when he'd taken her home. The younger woman hadn't stopped talking once during the twenty-minute drive to the place she shared with her sister. Her twin sister. The one who'd stolen a candy bar at the local corner store when she was seven and then told everyone she was Kinsley when she'd gotten caught. He'd also learned that the sister had wet the bed until she was six years old and that Kinsley hadn't gone on any sleepovers until her sister had mastered bladder control because Kinsley wouldn't go anywhere without her.

It had been way too much information, and he'd tuned out so thoroughly that he hadn't even heard her when she'd pointed out her apartment building.

And now as they were getting ready to mount their brooms, she was rambling about her Nana's incontinence problems.

"You would just not believe the smell, Niko. I'm telling you, I love her to pieces, but if she doesn't start wearing adult diapers, I'm gonna have to threaten to put her in a home."

Niko cleared his throat. "Does she live with you and your sister?"

"Oh no," she said, shaking her head. "She has her own place. But you know how it is. When we go over there, there's no ignoring the smell."

"Uh-huh." Niko kicked off, grateful to get out of the

conversation. Despite the fact that he hadn't been in the mood to go on a broom ride earlier, he had to admit that the heaviness that had been weighing him down had suddenly disappeared, and there wasn't much that made him feel better than flying over the Salish Sea in the Pacific Northwest.

Kinsley let out a cry of surprise, causing him to glance back. She was on her broom, wobbling a bit.

Niko quickly swung around, flying up close to her. "Level your handle!"

She glanced at him with wide, terrified eyes.

"Lean forward and level the broom handle," he ordered again. "Just like this." He demonstrated what he meant and watched her closely.

She tentatively leaned forward and immediately the broom took off, speeding over the bay.

He hurried to catch up with her, frustration bubbling over. Had the woman never ridden a broom before? "Pull up slightly!"

Her eyes were terrified, but she did as she was told, and as she slowed, her expression eased, an obvious look of relief on her young face.

"Follow me," he said and made a gentle turn to head back to the shore.

Thankfully, Kinsley did as he asked, but when they landed, she didn't get her feet under her and ended up dragging her legs, causing her to flail and fall off the broom. Without a rider, the broom just fell on the rocky beach, landing with a dull thud while Kinsley moaned and curled into herself.

"Kinsley!" Niko called as he ran over and crouched beside her. He placed a light hand on her shoulder. "Are you all right?"

She moaned again and rolled over, staring up at him, blinking away tears. "I'm okay," she said as she tried to push herself up. "I just… lost control there for a minute."

Niko helped her into a sitting position. "Have you ever ridden a broom before?"

"Of course. My sister and I had a lesson when we were like eight, I think."

"So just once?" Niko asked.

"Yeah, but it's like riding a bike, right?"

"Seems maybe not," he said, shaking his head. Especially when she hadn't ridden one since she was a kid. And certainly not one that had the capacity to go as fast or as high as the one she had been riding.

She shifted, trying to get her feet under her and stand. Wincing, she released the pressure off her left foot and reached for her ankle. "That's gonna make it hard to stand at work."

"You need a healer," he said, wrapping his arm around her waist, trying to support her.

"No, no. It's just a minor sprain," Kinsley said, leaning into him. "What I need to do is get right back on that broom."

"I don't think that's—" Niko started.

But Kinsley cut him off. "I'm not a quitter. I'm certain I can master this if I just give it another shot."

There was no way Niko was letting that happen. She'd nearly fallen from fifty feet in the air, and she'd ended the trip with a spectacular crash landing. "Not tonight," he said firmly. "Not on my watch."

"But—" A gust of wind drowned out her protest and was followed by a sudden rain shower.

Kinsley just looked at him and nodded.

He grabbed both their brooms, and then without a word, he hauled her into his arms and made a run for it to their vehicles.

In no time, he had her tucked into her red Kia Soul. Before he shut her door he asked, "Can you drive?"

"It's my left foot. Yes. I can drive," she said. "I'll just go home and put ice on it. I'm sure it'll be fine."

"You really should go see a healer," he said again.

"That costs money. Ice will be fine." She smiled up at him. "Thank you for saving me. You're a hero, you know."

He rolled his eyes. "No, I'm not." If he was, he'd have put her in his truck and taken her to the healer himself. But he just couldn't bring himself to do anything more than wish her a good night.

"Goodnight, Niko. Maybe we can try this again sometime," she said.

He gave her a noncommittal smile and shut her door. He watched as she pulled out of the parking space and out onto Main Street. At least she appeared to be adept at handling her vehicle. That was great news, because all he wanted to do was go home, take a hot shower, down a whiskey, and forget this day ever happened.

With the rain still pouring down, Niko ran to his truck and climbed in. On his way out of town, he slowed as he passed Brooms that Vroom and looked up at the glowing light in the apartment upstairs. If he had his way, he'd be with Indigo at that very moment, dragging her to the shower with him.

# CHAPTER 5

"YOU DID WHAT?" Prim asked, staring at Indigo like she'd lost her mind. They were sitting out front of The Witch's Brew, the coffee shop and café that was two doors down from Brooms that Vroom.

Indigo glanced away, pretending she didn't hear her sister chastising her.

"She told the man she's clearly head over heels for to date her new employee," Lily explained. "Because she's an idiot. I mean, who does that?"

Indigo scowled at her sisters. The two looked like twins with their identical incredulous expressions. It didn't help that they both were blond with blue eyes and had the same delicate features. If she hadn't been there to see that they were born ten months apart, she never would have believed that they didn't share the same birthday. "Stop giving me shit about this. I'm not going to date Niko. So why should I care if he dates someone else?"

"A twenty-one-year-old?" Lily asked, shaking her head. "Please. Niko isn't going to get serious with a college girl. Have you met the man? He's the oldest thirty-three-year-old I've ever met. The man reads for fun and heads home by nine when Brax gets together with him for boys' night."

Indigo couldn't help the laugh that sprang from her lips. "You make him sound like he's eighty."

"I'm just saying that he's not gonna be a good fit for a college girl," Lily said. "You, however, have been known to turn in early in your old age."

"Old? Watch it, little Easton," Indigo said, though she couldn't deny the truth of her sister's words. When she wasn't on a date, or hooking up with a hot guy in Florida, she was known to turn into a pumpkin when the clock struck nine p.m. "Those are fighting words."

Her two youngest sisters smirked at each other, but then Prim turned a serious gaze on her. "We worry about you, Indy. You can't keep pushing people away because of your past. It's not healthy."

"Okay, that's enough." Indigo stood. "As much as I love to be grilled on my nonexistent love life, it's time for me to get to the shop before the college girl shows up."

"Wait!" Prim grasped Indigo's wrist, stopping her. "I forgot to tell you why I wanted to meet this morning."

Indigo raised her eyebrows. "You signed me and Niko up for dance classes down at the mansion?"

"No, but that's a really good idea. I'll get right on that." Prim gave her a wicked smile, transforming her sweet face into one of pure mischief.

A sudden image of Indigo being twirled around the

mansion above the bluff that had been turned into a community center flashed in Indigo's head. It was a welcome image that she liked far too much for her own good. She glared at her sister. "Don't you dare."

Prim laughed. "Okay, fine. If I agree not to sign you two up for dance lessons, can I count on you to help with the masquerade ball fundraiser for the new Befana Bay library?"

"There's a new Befana Bay library?" Indigo asked, confused. "It's not at the old library, is it?"

"You mean Gothic Books?" Lily asked, already nodding. "Yes, actually. Dante wanted to honor the original building, so he's dedicating part of the upstairs as a local library."

"That's…" Indigo's eyes stung with tears, taking her off guard. She let out a soft chuckle. "I don't know why I'm getting choked up. That's just so wonderful. Of course I'll help. Just let me know what you need."

Prim's smile widened. "Lily and I just came up with the idea last night, so we're in the initial planning stages, but we'll need your help to cast some spells and work on advertising the event."

"Sure." Indigo squeezed her sister's hand. "I'm happy to. Let me know when and I'll be there."

Lily and Prim both stood, giving Indigo a hug before sitting back down to finish their coffees while Indigo took off to get the shop ready to open for the day.

"INDIGO?" Kinsley asked as she limped up to the counter, holding one of the brooms from the stockroom.

"Yeah?" After showing Kinsley around, she'd asked her to check in some new stock in the back room. Her eyes focused on Kinsley's left foot. "What happened? Did you hurt yourself?"

"Oh, it's nothing. I twisted my ankle last night and have a minor sprain. The ibuprofen has just worn off. I'll take a couple more pills and will be fine."

"You have a sprained ankle and you're walking around?" Indigo gasped out. "Why didn't you tell me? Come behind the counter and sit. You shouldn't be standing on that all day." She held her hand out to the other woman and guided her to the stool behind the counter. "Sit."

After Kinsley did as she was told, Indigo grabbed the empty trash can and turned it over. "Prop your foot on this."

"I'll be fine," Kinsley insisted even as she followed Indigo's orders. "Really. It's not a big deal."

"You're limping. That's enough for me. I won't have you putting pressure on it while it heals. Understand?"

"Yes, ma'am." Kinsley smiled gratefully at her. "Thank you. I could have hobbled through it, but I have to admit that it's aching."

"No thanks necessary. All we're doing here is selling brooms and a little magic. No need to exacerbate an injury." She nodded to the broom still in Kinsley's hand. "Now, did you have a question about that?"

She glanced at the broom as if she'd forgotten she was holding it and then turned her attention back to Indigo. "These aren't spelled, right?"

Indigo shook her head. "Nope. I do that myself."

Kinsley's eyes lit up. "Can I be there when you do that?

I'd love to watch you in action. Learn a thing or two from you."

A prickle of unease washed over Indigo. Unless she was with her sisters and grandmother, she was always a little hesitant to work her magic around anyone else and preferred to work alone. But she had made an exception for Luke, her assistant who'd been working with her for the last five years. She supposed she'd have to do the same for Kinsley since she'd be working there for the foreseeable future.

There was no real reason to be so private about her spells. She wasn't doing anything that couldn't be looked up in an advanced spell book. It was just that after the incident she'd had in college, she'd hated casting around anyone other than her trusted circle.

"Sure," she forced herself to say. "But not that one. Let's start with one of the beginner brooms. That one is for advanced riders and requires a lot of energy to get the spell right."

"There are different performance levels?" Kinsley asked, her eyes wide.

"Of course," Indigo said with a chuckle. "There are ones that might as well have training wheels. And then there are the ones that are as responsive as a high-performance sports car." She nodded to the gorgeous, sleek onyx one in Kinsley's hand. "Once I'm done with that one, it'll go zero to sixty in 2.2 seconds flat. It's really for the most experienced riders."

"Hmm, maybe that was my problem," Kinsley mumbled to herself.

"Problem?" Indigo walked out from behind the counter to give her employee her full attention.

"Oh." Kinsley waved a hand and let out an embarrassed laugh. "I went on a broom ride last night and borrowed my sister's broom. She rides all the time, but honestly, I haven't been on one since I was a kid. And let's just say it didn't go well. If it hadn't been for Niko, I'd have likely crashed hard into the bay." She swallowed hard. "Who knows what would have happened to me?"

"Niko?" Indigo asked and immediately clamped her mouth shut. The woman had just told her she'd almost had a catastrophic crash on a broom, and all Indigo could think about was the fact that she'd been with the man Indigo refused to date.

"Yeah. He invited me to go along with him on his ride." She gave Indigo a tentative smile. "It was okay that I went, right? I mean, you two…" The young woman bit her bottom lip. "I figured he wouldn't have asked if you two were… involved."

"We're definitely not involved," Indigo said firmly. "In fact, I told him to invite you."

"You did?" she asked, her voice rising a few octaves.

"Yeah, he asked me, but I had to turn him down, so…"

Kinsley beamed. "That was very kind of you. He's really dreamy."

He definitely was that. And sexy. And the only one who'd caught Indigo's attention in the past five years. But that was beside the point. "It was nothing. Hopefully, you had a good time despite the malfunction that almost dumped you in the bay."

"Well, good time might be stretching it," she said as she glanced away.

She definitely had Indigo's full attention now. "You didn't have a good time?"

"No. Not really." She wrinkled her nose. "I couldn't master the broom, and like I said, Niko had to help me get it under control. And then when we went in for the landing, that's when I fell off and hurt my ankle. To say that I was mortified would be an understatement. I suggested I get right back on. You know, that whole thing about getting back on the bike... That stuck with me as a kid. But Niko wouldn't let me. Then it started to rain and he put me in my car and told me to go home."

"Ouch. That sounds awful," Indigo said, cringing for her. As much as she hadn't wanted to hear that Niko had spent the evening with her, she had to admit that she was relieved the date had crashed and burned, so to speak.

"It was. I've never been so humiliated." Kinsley sighed as she thumped her head on the front counter. "And on top of that, I was so nervous I rambled about the most embarrassing stuff. I'll never be able to show my face around him again."

This time Indigo did chuckle. She patted her new employee on the shoulder and said, "I'm sure it wasn't that horrible."

"You have no idea." Kinsley made a face and then handed the broom over.

Indigo took it to the back room, grabbed a couple of the beginner brooms, and made her way back up to the front counter. "Okay, since it's slow, let me show you how I do this, and then you can practice on the second one. You game?"

Kinsley sat up straight. "Really? That would be amaaaazing."

"Sure. Why not?" Indigo wasn't sure what possessed her to make the offer to the other woman. Maybe she was feeling a little sorry for her. It sounded like she'd had a night she'd just as soon forget.

"Okay, I'm ready. Where do we start?"

Indigo laughed, kind of loving how eager her new employee was. It was nice to have a little excitement in the shop. She laid the broom on the counter and then grabbed her salt and a few herbs from a locked cabinet.

"Do you keep the herbs locked up because they are dangerous or because they are expensive?" Kinsley asked.

"Both. They aren't especially dangerous, but if someone without knowledge tried to use them, it could go south quickly. It's just more responsible to keep the raw herbs locked away."

Kinsley nodded, suddenly looking serious as she waited.

"Okay, first we make a salt circle around the broom. That's just a safety precaution. Though it does help concentrate the spell so I don't have to use as much energy. So don't skip that step."

"Got it."

Indigo made the salt circle and then retrieved the herbs that would seal the spell. Once she ground them together with her pestle and mortar, she placed the bowl next to the broom. "Okay, now that the herbs are ready, it's time for the incantation. Once the spell is set, we burn the herbs and sprinkle the ashes on the handle."

"Seems easy enough," Kinsley said.

"It's not difficult, you just have to focus your energy." Indigo closed her eyes, pictured the broom in her mind's eye and then raised her arms and said, "Air and earth, I call on the spirit of the Easton witches and ask for strength to compel this broom to fly. May the spirit bless this broom with energy and life to keep its riders safe. From east to west and north to south, please protect this broom and its riders. Three to one and one to three, here my call, so mote it be!"

Magic pooled at the ends of Indigo's fingers, and she immediately placed her hands on the broom, infusing the magic into the wood. Then she stared at the herbs in the bowl and ordered, "Ignite!"

The herbs instantly turned to ashes, and Indigo called, "Scatter!"

The ash rose in the air, spread out, and then gently fell onto the broom handle, making it glow for just a moment before the light winked out.

Indigo grinned at Kinsley. "All done. Are you ready to try?"

Kinsley blinked at her. "Now?"

"There's no time like the present." Indigo took the freshly spelled broom from the counter and placed it behind the register. It wouldn't be ready to stock until they test rode it. "Grab the other broom and put it in the circle."

Once the broom was laid out, Kinsley asked, "Do I need to redo the salt circle?"

"Not unless it gets damaged. This one looks fine." She handed her charge the herbs and instructed her to follow the recipe. Five minutes later, the herbs were ready to go. "Excellent. Now it's your turn to try the incantation. Keep focused on the broom the entire time with the intent on directing your magic toward it."

"But I can't call on the Easton witches, can I?" Kinsley looked worried. "I have to use my own line, right?"

"Normally, yes. But when you're in my shop, my line is available to you as well. Use whichever comes easiest to you while you're learning. Mine is pretty powerful just because of our family line."

"I know. I can feel it. It's more intense than mine. Probably because my great-aunt Bertha denounced her witchy side and tried to curse my grandmother. It really put a dark mark on the family energy."

"She tried to curse your grandmother?" Indigo asked, pressing a hand to her heart.

"Yeah. It was ugly." Kinsley shuddered. "But she landed in the clink for it, so I guess she got what she deserved."

Indigo wasn't sure what to say to that. Her new employee certainly had a way of blurting things out that took Indigo off guard.

"So I'll use the Easton energy," Kinsley said, closing her eyes. "I place my hands on the broom?"

"Not yet. Raise them in the air, but keep your mind focused on the broom as you say the incantation."

"Okay." Kinsley raised her arms in the air and repeated the incantation. A whisper of magic appeared at her fingertips, making Indigo frown. There should have been more of a spark.

"Try the chant again. This time imagine you're pouring magic into the broom," Indigo said.

Kinsley nodded, and a few seconds later her fingers were glowing with magic.

"Perfect. Now grab the broom handle and direct your magic into it."

"On it." Kinsley gripped the broom and then screwed her face up in frustration as she tried, but failed, over and over to get the magic to take. She opened her eyes and stared at Indigo. "What am I doing wrong?"

Indigo chewed on her bottom lip before walking behind her new employee and covering Kinsley's hands with her own. The magic was strong and pulsing with energy. There was no reason it should be blocked.

Concentrating on the magic flowing from Kinsley, Indigo helped nudge it toward the broom handle. "Feel that? I'm using my will to send the magic to the broom. Can you do that?"

"I don't—oh! There it is." The magic poured into the broom and Kinsley's face lit with a happy grin. "That was amazing!"

"You're not done yet. Burn the herbs and then seal the spell to the broom," Indigo instructed.

"Right." Kinsley stared at the bowl of herbs for just a moment before they went up in flames. And just as Indigo had done, her apprentice manipulated the ashes with her mind and instructed them to cover the broom. It glowed just like the previous one had, and then the flash of light disappeared suddenly.

"Well done!" Indigo cried. "You did it on the first try."

"Well technically, second, but who's counting." Kinsley let out a whoop of excitement as she stood suddenly and then immediately winced. "Oops. I forgot all about my ankle." She rotated it as she eyed the door. "If I can hobble out there, can we test these out?"

Indigo didn't have the heart to say no, so she nodded and said, "Just take it easy, okay?"

"Aye, aye, Captain." Kinsley grabbed the broom she'd spelled and hobbled out quicker than Indigo imagined she could.

After a moment, she joined her employee outside, ready to test the brooms. But just as she was climbing on, she heard a shout from across the street. And when she looked up, she spotted a woman who was staring at her arms as black dagger tattoos appeared out of nowhere on her forearms and then seemed to light with fire, making the woman scream bloody murder.

Indigo dropped her broom and ran.

# CHAPTER 6

"WHAT THE HELL IS THAT?" Brax exclaimed as he started to stride toward the front window of his outdoor shop.

Niko turned his attention from the fancy new kayak he'd been considering as an upgrade and glanced past his friend at the woman across the street and two stores up.

The doorbell chimed as Dante suddenly appeared, and through labored breath as if he'd just been running, he gasped out, "Help! Someone's on fire!"

"Call 911!" Niko jumped into action, rushing outside to help the woman whose arms were covered in flames.

He ran flat out, already pulling his sweatshirt over his head, intending to use it to put the fire out, but before he could reach her, Indigo was there, magic pouring out of her fingertips. She'd grabbed onto the woman and an ice blue light of magic was quickly quenching the flames.

Niko came to a stop a few feet from the women, not wanting to interrupt as Indigo seemed to have it under control but making sure he was ready just in case he was needed. Her magic was impressive, and although he'd witnessed powerful witches before, he'd had no idea that Indigo possessed that kind of power. He supposed it shouldn't be that much of a shock considering she was a descendant of the Befana witches, but it was one thing to know a family had a strong magical line; it was another to witness it.

"Shine the light on the darkness," Indigo cried, her voice hoarse and full of emotion. "Release the chains that hold this woman. Feed it back to me. I call on the power of the Befana bloodline to reclaim the darkness and send the light. Release the darkness, let me be the beacon that makes this right!"

The ice blue magic sizzled and disappeared just as the flames reared back to life, only instead of engulfing the woman, they jumped from her arms onto Indigo's.

Horrified, Niko lunged, throwing his sweatshirt over Indigo as he tackled her to the ground, quickly patting out the flames.

"Oh my goddess! Oh my goddess!" the woman Indigo had saved said over and over again through her sobs.

Niko barely spared her a glance as he rolled off Indigo and inspected her skin for burn marks. He stared, frowning at her arms. They were red, but not blistered. However, that wasn't what had shocked him.

Right there on the inside of both forearms were a pair of matching dagger tattoos. Ones that hadn't been there a few days before.

He picked up one arm, studying the tattoo. Nothing

48

about it indicated that it was fresh ink, though it was hard to tell since her arm was red from the fire. But that didn't explain the lack of puffiness.

He looked up into her glazed eyes and frowned. "Indigo? Are you okay?"

She blinked at him and then let out a small groan as she tried to push herself up.

He wrapped an arm around her, helping her into a sitting position.

"Thanks," she said, her voice cracking as if her vocal chords were singed.

"You saved me," the woman said, moving to crouch beside Indigo. Her arms had zero indication that she'd just been burned. It appeared that Indigo hadn't only saved her from the fire, she'd managed to heal whatever damage had been done as well. "Thank you. You're a goddess."

Indigo turned to the woman, her eyes darkening. "Who spelled you?"

"Spelled?" the woman asked as she suddenly got to her feet and shook her head. "Why would someone spell me?"

"I don't—" Indigo suddenly went limp in Niko's arms.

"Indigo? Hey," Niko said softly, pressing his palm to her face. Panic started to set in when she didn't respond. He quickly laid her back on the ground and checked her vitals. Her pulse was steady, and she didn't appear to be having trouble breathing. Both were good signs. But she was still unconscious.

Sirens sounded in the distance.

Niko glanced up, looking for the emergency vehicle. It was then he noticed that Kinsley, Brax, and Dante were all standing behind him, keeping a growing crowd from invading his and Indigo's space. But the woman Indigo had saved was nowhere to be found. "Where'd she go?"

"Who?" Kinsley asked.

"The woman. The one Indigo saved. I need to question her," Niko said, frustrated. "Surely she's here somewhere, waiting for medical attention." Though he hadn't seen any obvious injuries.

Dante shook his head. "After Indigo asked who spelled her, she disappeared into the crowd. I think she took off."

Damn. Normally Niko would do his best to chase down anyone involved with an illegal spell, but he couldn't just leave Indigo. His body wouldn't physically let him.

"Lily will be here in a second," Brax said after glancing at his phone.

"Good." Niko stayed by Indigo's side, refusing to move even when the paramedics arrived.

One of them took her vitals and frowned. "How long has she been out?"

"A few minutes," Niko said. "She used a lot of magic. The effort exhausted her, but she was initially alert. And then she suddenly just went limp."

"Spell exhaustion," Lily said appearing from behind Braxton. "This has happened before."

The paramedic looked up at Indigo's sister. "How often?"

"Lately, not often at all. But when she was in college, it was more common. The more stressed she was, the more often it occurred," Lily explained. "I'm positive all she needs is some rest."

"I can't just leave an unconscious woman," the paramedic said. "I'll need to take her to the hospital to be checked out."

Niko was ready to help the man load Indigo into the ambulance, but Lily shook her head. "She'd hate that." Then Lily dropped down and pressed both palms to Indigo's cheeks and quietly said, "Time to wake up, sis. You're causing a bit of a scene." A spark of magic rippled off Lily's fingers but was gone just as quickly as it appeared.

Indigo's eyes flickered open. She took a moment to orient herself, blinking and looking around. Then she focused on Lily. "It happened again?"

Her sister nodded solemnly. "I wouldn't let them take you to the hospital."

"Good," she croaked out and again tried to push herself up.

"Indigo wait," Niko said, pressing a light hand to her shoulder. "The last time you sat up, you passed out."

"I'm all right," she said. "Or I will be." But her hands were shaking, and she was white as a sheet.

"Niko," Lily said. "Can you help her up?"

"I really think—" he started, but when Indigo grabbed his arm, her grip was a lot stronger than he expected it to be.

"I just need some rest and an herbal infusion. Can you help me back to my apartment?"

Niko glanced at the paramedic.

The young man looked at Indigo. "Are you refusing care?"

"Yes," she said solemnly. "But only because I've been here

before. All that will happen if you take me in is a big bill after they hydrate me. I can do that at home."

"Will you let me take your blood pressure one more time?" the EMT asked.

She nodded as she closed her eyes and slumped against Niko.

The EMT got to work, and once he got his reading, he frowned. "It's lower than I'd like, but it's not in the danger zone. I'm advising you to keep an eye on this as well as your other vitals."

"I will make sure of it," Lily told the EMT. "Thank you. I appreciate you looking after my sister."

The paramedics packed up their supplies and stepped back as Niko helped Indigo to her feet. When she stumbled, he swept her up into his arms and started moving toward her apartment.

"I can walk," she said weakly.

"Maybe, but I'm not risking it," he said softly. "Just let me do this, all right?"

Indigo rested her head against his chest and mumbled, "Okay."

Lily fell into step beside them and said, "I'll take care of the shop. Just get her home."

"Will do," Niko said as he hurried away from the crowd.

When he reached the door of her apartment, he found it was locked and said, "Do you have the key on you?"

"Hmm?" She didn't open her eyes and snuggled in closer.

"To your apartment. It's locked."

"We're at my apartment?" she mumbled as her eyes fluttered open.

"Yes. You need to rest. Do I need to go get your key from downstairs?"

"No." She pressed her hand to the doorknob, and immediately the door opened.

He frowned. "Did you just use magic?"

"No." She shook her head slightly and muttered something about the knob being spelled to her touch.

He carried her inside, heading straight for her bedroom. After gently lying her on her perfectly made-up bed, he sat beside her on the cheerful sunflower print bedspread and brushed her dark hair out of her eyes. "You were really something today the way you saved that woman."

Her brow wrinkled while she shook her head slightly, looking pained.

"You were. That was some impressive magic, Indigo. And being on the Magical Task Force, I feel like I've seen it all."

Her eyes flew open as panic flashed on her face. "What happened to the woman?"

"I don't know. She disappeared once you passed out," he said. "Did you know her?"

"No." Her voice sounded wary. "But I know the spell." She was staring across the room, her expression blank. Then in an emotionless tone she added, "It's my fault. I did this."

"Did what?" he asked, feeling uneasy, like he wasn't going to like the answer.

But instead of answering, Indigo's eyes closed again and her body went limp with sleep.

"Indigo?" he asked softly.

She didn't move, and when he pressed a soft hand to her cheek, she muttered something unintelligible.

Satisfied that she hadn't passed out again and was just sleeping, he got up and went to the other room. After finding water for her bedside table, he took a seat on her couch and settled in for the night. There was zero chance he was leaving until he was certain that Indigo wouldn't suffer any backlash for the magic she'd dispelled to save the stranger.

About an hour after Indigo fell asleep, there was a soft knock on the door.

Niko answered it, finding Lily on the other side, holding a bottle that looked like a homemade potion.

"How's the patient?" Lily asked as she strode into the apartment.

"Asleep."

She nodded. "I figured as much. Has she said anything?"

"Not much. Just that she knew the spell and that it was somehow her fault," he said, wondering if Lily knew anything about that.

Lily chewed on her bottom lip as she stared toward the closed door of the bedroom.

"Do you know what she meant by that?" Niko asked, suspecting that Lily knew a lot more than she was willing to share.

"Yes." Lily gave him a sad, sympathetic smile. "But that's her story to tell." She walked into the attached kitchen and put the potion in the fridge. "You can go now. I'll stay with her tonight."

"I'm staying," he said simply, prepared to pull out the

Magical Task Force agent card. He had no doubt that the spell that set that woman on fire was an illegal one, and he did have a moral obligation to investigate it. However, if he was honest with himself, that wasn't the reason he wasn't going anywhere.

Lily eyed him for a long moment, and he wondered if she was going to try to throw him out. But then she just nodded once and said, "I figured you might say that. Just..." She grimaced and shook her head again.

"Just what?" he asked, wondering what Lily thought about him refusing to leave. It wasn't something someone would do who had only taken someone out one time. Did she suspect that Niko had it bad for her sister? Or did she just think he was the protective type?

"Just be patient with her." Lily squeezed his arm gently and walked to the door. Before she left, she said, "When she wakes up, give her the potion. It will help restore her energy."

"I will."

The door closed gently behind Lily, leaving Niko alone with his thoughts. He took a seat in a chair that offered a clear view of the bedroom door and only then let himself really think about what he'd done that day.

An illegal spell had been cast and he hadn't called it in.

Why?

He knew why. Because Indigo had known how to counter it, and that was a major red flag. He needed to talk to her before he made his report. *If* he made a report.

Indigo slept the rest of the afternoon away. He eventually ordered takeout for dinner, making sure to get enough for Indigo in case she woke up hungry. He doubted it, but he wanted to be prepared.

He'd just finished his grilled cheese and tomato soup combo from The Salt Circle when he heard Indigo cry out from the other room. He jumped up and ran to her side, finding her thrashing on the bed, her eyes still closed.

"Indigo?" he asked as he gently placed a hand on her shoulder.

She jerked in her sleep, swatting at him as she cried, "Get away!"

There was no doubt this was a nightmare. He had to do something to bring her out of it.

Keeping his hands to himself so he didn't alarm her again, he kept his voice low and steady as he said, "Hey now. It's okay, Indigo. You're safe. You're here in your apartment and safe. Wake up. It's okay. I promise. Just wake up."

She didn't open her eyes, but the thrashing stopped and her breathing leveled out.

He was about to leave when her hand shot out and grabbed his wrist, stopping him.

"Do you want me to stay?" he asked.

She didn't respond, but her grip tightened slightly. He took it as a yes and sat back down on the bed. After a moment, his own eyes got heavy and he laid down next to her, careful to keep a bit of distance between them. But that was short-lived, because Indigo immediately rolled into him, wrapping her arm across his chest and resting her head on his shoulder.

He froze, wondering if she knew what she was doing. But when she let out a contented sigh, he curled his arm around her shoulders and decided he'd hold her for as long as she would let him.

"GOOD MORNING," a soft voice said, rousing Niko out of his slumber.

He opened his eyes, squinting in the morning sunlight. His lips curved into a small smile as he looked down at the rumpled, sleepy woman who was still snuggled next to him. There was nothing like waking up to the gorgeous woman in his arms. It felt far too good, and he knew he should try to put some distance between them, but instead, he kissed the top of her head and said, "Good morning."

She was quiet for a few moments before she said, "Thanks for staying with me."

"I'd stay every night if you'd let me," he teased.

Indigo flinched, and he instantly regretted the words.

"Hey, I'm sorry," he said, giving her a look of concern. "That was just a little bit of flirting. I didn't mean to make you uncomfortable."

"I'm not uncomfortable," she said with a humorless laugh. "That's the problem. I'm entirely *too* comfortable." She pushed herself up into a sitting position and then when she noticed her hands were shaking slightly, she pressed her head into her hands. "Did Lily bring me a potion?"

"She did. I'll go get it. Do you want food, too?" he asked, already missing her warm embrace. "You've been out since yesterday afternoon and must be starving."

"No, just the potion for now. Thank you."

He hurried into her kitchen and grabbed the bottle that Lily had dropped off the night before and was back in a flash. After handing her the potion, he took a seat in a chair that was in the corner and waited as she drained the green liquid.

Color instantly came back into her cheeks, and she was no longer shaking.

"Hey, that stuff appears to be a miracle potion. I wish I'd had something like that the last time I went to the bar with Brax and Dante. I'm pretty sure I drank more beer than an Irishman on St Patty's Day."

"I bet you felt fabulous the next morning," she said with a snicker. "Sadly, this potion isn't the one for that, but my grandmother does make something just for those types of occasions."

"Bethany makes hangover potions?" he asked with a laugh. "Somehow, I guess that's not surprising."

"If she were looking for a career, she could make a mint on that stuff. Instead, she just does the potions for friends and family." She raised the bottle. "That's where Lily got this. Our grandmother is a very gifted witch."

"So I've heard." He leaned forward, and although he didn't want to, he began asking the questions he was obligated to ask. "How did you know how to reverse that spell yesterday, Indigo?"

She glanced away but not before her jaw tightened.

"I know you don't want to talk about this, but it's my job and I have to ask."

Indigo turned her tired gaze on him and said, "I'm sure there's a file on me somewhere. You can look it up. But before you start thinking I'm responsible for this, you should know that I haven't dealt with that type of magic since I was a senior in college. That spell won't be traced back to me because I make a point of staying far away from it."

He sat back, stunned by the venom in her tone. Then he eyed her curiously. "This is why you don't date law enforcement."

She let out a bark of humorless laughter. "Because criminals don't date the law, right? That's what you're thinking?"

Remaining calm, he held her gaze for a long moment before answering. "I never said you were a criminal."

"But you were thinking it." The defiance in her tone was full of righteous anger.

"I wouldn't bet on that," he said. "People make mistakes all the time, especially when they're young. That doesn't mean those mistakes should follow someone around for the rest of their life." He could only imagine what kind of trouble she'd gotten up to as a young adult. But the woman he knew now? She was careful, and he hadn't known her to practice any magic that wasn't a run of the mill charm meant to spell objects for fun or entertainment. The harmless kind.

"It's accurate to say that people make mistakes," she said evenly. "Maybe that's true for me, too. Or maybe it isn't. But I'm not going to talk about them, and I'm certainly not going to make a statement to law enforcement without a lawyer present. I think it's time for you to go, Niko." Indigo climbed off her bed and moved to stand next to the window, barely registering the sun sparkling off the bay

He couldn't argue with that. She certainly was entitled to someone from the magical council. And she was smart to say so. Still, he couldn't resist asking one more question. "Can you just tell me if you have ever seen that woman before?"

She pressed her lips together into a tight line, and for a moment he thought she was going to refuse to answer. But then her shoulders slumped slightly, and she shook her head. "No. I don't know who spelled her or why or how she ended up in front of my shop."

He nodded. "That's what I thought. Will you do me a favor?"

She shrugged one shoulder. "Depends on what it is."

"Let me know if you see her again… or anyone using that magic."

Indigo glanced away, but then nodded once. "Now go. I have things to do today before I open the store."

For some reason he hadn't imagined her going into work that day, but that was shortsighted since Indigo was a small business owner. Taking time off had to be planned for.

He walked over to her, standing close until she looked up at him. He tucked a lock of her dark hair behind her ear and said, "I'm glad you're feeling better."

Indigo searched his gaze, her expression unreadable. Then she lifted up on her toes and gave him a sweet kiss on the cheek. "Thanks for keeping an eye on me."

"Always," he said and then left before he lost himself and gave her a kiss she wouldn't soon forget.

# CHAPTER 7

INDIGO STARED at her apartment door, wishing Niko would walk back in. When she'd woken in his arms that morning, she'd had a brief moment of pure happiness. She'd wanted to live in his arms forever. But then reality had kicked in, and not only had her hands started to shake, but her head had also started to pound.

Thank the goddess and her grandmother for the potion. While she still didn't feel her best, she certainly was functional, and that was pretty much all she could ask for after burning herself out the day before.

What she really wanted to do was have a leisurely breakfast with Niko and enjoy his company while she put everything else out of her mind. She knew that if she called, he'd come back over, but that was out of the question. He'd want answers. Answers she didn't have. And until she knew who had spelled that woman and why, she couldn't tell him.

Not this time.

That was a mistake she wasn't willing to make again.

She turned from the door and went into the kitchen. Suddenly she was ravenous, and her stomach felt like it was eating itself. When she opened the fridge, she found the takeout that Niko had ordered the night before. And even though it was morning, she heated up the soup and the grilled cheese and ate it as if she hadn't eaten in a week.

"Thank you, Niko," she said as she cleaned up her kitchen and grabbed a flavored water from her fridge. "That was just what I needed."

A half hour later, she was showered, sitting at her desk in her office, and ready to face her day. Except instead of checking inventory and invoices, all she could think about was the spell that she'd neutralized the day before.

Who had cast it, and why?

Where had they learned it?

And why had they targeted the woman who just happened to be across the street from her store?

Her skin started to tingle. And not in a good way. She had to stand and shake out her limbs, trying to dispel the feeling.

It didn't work, and she found herself pacing her office.

Every time she passed the safe under her desk, she paused and stared at it. The pull to revisit her past was strong. It had been years since she'd looked at those journals. Since she'd let herself think about everything that had gone down her last year in college.

A dull ache took up residence in her chest, and she unconsciously rubbed at her breastbone.

THE WITCH'S LOST SPELL

Her movements were mechanical as she moved toward the safe. As if she were on autopilot, she spun the combination until she heard the telltale *click* and the safe popped open.

Her hand was shaking again when she reached in and pulled the leatherbound journal from the top of the stack. The one she hadn't touched in over a decade. The leather was cool to the touch, but as her hand tightened around it, she could almost feel the magic that was written within.

She sat at her desk, running her fingers over her journal until the compulsion was too much and she finally cracked the book open.

Immediately the memories rushed in, her present fading as she was consumed by the past.

*"INDIGO!" Tricia called. "Look, it's working."*

*"Finally," Indigo said, staring down at the now tattooed daggers on her forearms. They were glowing with magic, just the way they were supposed to. "I knew if we just kept at it, we'd get there."*

*They were in their apartment, working on their senior project, one that every witch was required to complete before they could graduate from Olympic Witches University. The goal was to create a spell or potion that would better society.*

*And this was the moment of truth.*

*Tricia and Indigo locked eyes as they chanted the incantation that would concentrate power into the tattoos that could be accessed later without having to invoke a chant or create a witch's circle. It was meant to make life easier for busy witches who* wanted to use a little magic to help them with their daily tasks while working or raising a family.

"Imprint the power into the daggers, let it be called on for future endeavors," the two of them chanted until finally an intense zap of magic sizzled over the tattoos, making them glow with what looked like fire.

Indigo sucked in a sharp breath but then immediately let it out when the fire extinguished.

"It's done! Oh. My. Goddess. We did it!" Tricia said as she threw her arms around Indigo, hugging her tightly.

Indigo felt an intense sense of pride at their accomplishment as she hugged her best friend and roommate, holding on for a long moment. They'd been working on this spell for months, and finally, all the hard work had paid off.

"Now we need to test it," Tricia said, her eyes sparkling with pride. "Go ahead. Give it a shot."

"What should I do first?" Indigo asked. "Clean the fireplace or the bathroom?"

Tricia glanced at the ashes that had accumulated around their hearth and nodded at the fireplace. "I just cleaned the bathroom a couple of days ago. Try for the fireplace."

"Okay. Keep your fingers crossed," Indigo said and then concentrated on the dagger tattoos that were inked on the insides of her forearms. Holding the images in her mind, she imagined the fireplace sparkling clean.

The tattoos came to life, glowing with a cool fire before they quickly winked out.

Indigo turned to watch the fireplace, waiting for all the ashes to be magically swept away.

But nothing happened.

*Indigo bit on her bottom lip, wondering what she'd done wrong. "Tricia—" she started but was cut off by her roommate's cry of alarm.*

*"Ouch! Son of a bitch!" Tricia called out. "What's happening to me?"*

*Indigo spun to find her friend staring down at her arms in horror. The dagger tattoos had appeared on her arms, but Tricia hadn't ever gotten a tattoo. Only Indigo had while they tested their spell. Then the images lit with the fire and Tricia froze, seemingly unable to move.*

*"Tricia, what's happening?" Indigo cried as she quickly moved to her friend's side.*

*The other woman ignored her as she focused on the fireplace. With robotic movements, she walked over to the hearth and started to scoop the ashes and toss them out the window.*

*"Tricia, stop! What's going on?"*

*But Tricia seemed not to hear Indigo and was singly focused on cleaning that fireplace. Horrified that it seemed she'd spelled her best friend to be some sort of robotic cleaning lady, Indigo hurried over and grabbed her arm. The magic pulsed beneath Tricia's skin, powerful and burning hot. Not knowing what else to do, Indigo latched onto the magic and ordered it back into her daggers.*

*Tricia screamed as the daggers once again lit up with flames.*

*Tears were streaming down Indigo's face as she held Tricia's hands and said, "Send the fire back to me! Clear Tricia of this spell! I call on the Befana ancestors to unring this bell!"*

*Blue magic poured from Indigo, covering Tricia's arms, and then suddenly the burning magic released Tricia and poured back into Indigo.*

*The magic overwhelmed her, making her feel as if she were burning from the inside out. And just when she thought she couldn't take it anymore, she collapsed and didn't wake up for forty-eight hours.*

*Once Indigo recovered, her faculty adviser informed her that the spell they'd created was one that possessed humans to do their deeds and that it was not only banned, but illegal. If they ever tried to do it again, both would be arrested.*

*Indigo had gladly agreed to put the spell in her vault and never mess with it again.*

*Three weeks later, someone got their hands on the spell, and that was when all hell broke loose.*

INDIGO SLAMMED the journal closed and quickly tossed it back in the safe. Memory lane wasn't a place she'd wanted to visit. Ever. But now that the spell had come back to haunt her, she hadn't had a choice.

The spell was here, and someone other than her had cast it. Now the only question was, who had access to that spell and why had they used it on the woman who'd been across from her shop?

She was certain she'd find out. She just hoped she'd figure it out before someone got seriously hurt.

# CHAPTER 8

"So that's it. You're giving up on Indigo after you had the one perfect date and then spent the night watching over her as she slept? That doesn't seem like you," Brax said as he picked up his burger.

"She's made it clear she doesn't want a relationship with an MTF agent," Niko said, his shoulders tense. "What am I going to do? Stand out front of her apartment window with a boombox and hope she changed her mind?"

"Ha! It could work. Women go crazy for that scene in the movie." Brax chuckled. "Just make sure you let me know when you do it so I can get video."

Niko flipped him off and then stared out at the bay, remembering what it felt like to be kayaking there just a few nights before. "Something tells me that she'd call the cops and then close the blinds on me, but we'll keep that tactic in my back pocket. I just wish I knew what happened in her past to make her distrust law enforcement so much."

"I wish I knew, man," Brax said. "But it's the one thing the Eastons never talk about."

"That figures." Niko let out a sardonic chuckle. "And here I thought that my job might actually help me get a date. It turns out, I couldn't have been more wrong."

Brax laughed. "You thought all you had to do was put a uniform on and the witches would be following you around like you were wearing a love charm?"

Niko blinked at him and then made a face. "No. I thought having someone who could protect them might be a plus."

He snorted. "Have you met the Easton sisters? I don't think they're exactly waiting around for a man to keep them safe. Between the four of them, I'm pretty sure they could level the entire town if they needed to."

"Solid point," Niko said, sounding dejected even to his own ears. He'd always been attracted to strong women. And Indigo Easton was no exception. That was why it surprised him that she was so averse to dating him because of his job.

"Maybe she just needs time to come around," Brax said. "You know, time to get to know you better and form some trust."

"Maybe," Niko said, but he wasn't holding his breath. Indigo had seemed pretty definitive, and he wasn't one to push it when a woman set her boundaries.

"Or you could just forget it and date someone else," Brax suggested.

"Like who?" Niko wasn't interested in anyone else, but he was curious to know who Brax thought he should date.

"Maybe your secret admirer," Brax said to Niko,

smirking over his mug of beer. His friend took a sip and then nodded toward a woman making her way toward them.

Niko swallowed a groan when he realized the woman was Kinsley, the one he'd recklessly invited on a broom ride after Indigo had rejected him. He'd let Indigo bait him into asking Kinsley out even though the college student was far too young for him and far too eager to date an older man. She couldn't have been a day over twenty-one. Meanwhile, he was in his thirties and had already spotted premature gray at his temples. "Has she already seen me?"

"Yep." Brax chuckled as he got up. "Gotta hit the head. Try not to end up on another date. At this rate, you'll be engaged by next month."

Niko flipped him off and wondered if anyone besides Lily would actually miss the other man if he suddenly disappeared.

"Hello, gorgeous," Kinsley said, flashing those wide amber eyes at him. "I really enjoyed that broom ride the other night. There's nowhere quite as romantic as Befana Bay under the moonlight. Especially when one gets caught in the rain."

"I could do without the rain," he said, trying to sound disinterested. "With the wind, I think it was a little too chilly for a ride."

"Then we should schedule a do-over, don't you think?" She slipped into the chair that Brax had been occupying just moments before and gazed at him with what he'd started to think of as heart eyes.

All his warning signals were going off. He needed to exit

this conversation ASAP. "Uh, that's probably not—" His phone buzzed with an incoming call. He let out a sigh of relief, and as he pulled his phone out of his pocket, he said, "Sorry, I have to take this."

When she didn't move from Brax's chair, he frowned at her. "Can you give me a moment?"

"Oh, sure." She hopped up and then moved about ten feet from the table, still watching him.

He ground his teeth before he answered the call. "Agent Morales."

"I hope you're ready to go back to work because I've got a case for you," Willa, his supervisor, said.

"Is it urgent or a cold case?" he asked, already pulling bills out of his wallet.

"Sort of both," she said. "I'm sending you the files now. Read them over and then interview the victim. Call if you have any questions."

"Got it." He hit End on his phone and looked up to find Brax standing at the table.

"I guess lunch is over," his friend said.

"Sorry, man. Duty calls." Niko stood, clapped his friend on the shoulder, and hurried out of the restaurant. He had a case to solve.

NIKO STARED at the files he'd printed out and swallowed the bile that rose up from the back of his throat. He'd seen more than his share of evil over the years. It was just part of the job. But this case was one of the ones that made him understand why some agents found themselves drowning in the bottom of a bottle.

His new case revolved around a witch who had been rescued from a burning building where she had been held captive and spelled into servitude. Unfortunately, the victim appeared to still be affected by the spell, so getting any information on who was responsible for the heinous crime had so far been difficult at best. It appeared she'd been compelled to keep her captor's identity secret. Now it was up to Niko to investigate.

He picked up his phone and called the number that was listed for the victim. The first thing he always did was conduct an interview.

"Bay View Hospital," a kind woman said when she answered.

He quickly introduced himself and asked if there was a way to talk to Polly Smart.

"I'm sorry, sir. Polly's family has barred visitors while she recovers," the administrator said.

"Even law enforcement? Can you please let them know I'm working on her case and would just like a few minutes."

She briefly put him on hold. When she came back on the line, she said, "Unfortunately, the family is adamant that she be left alone to heal. They said she already gave a statement."

"I understand. Thanks for checking." He ended the call slightly frustrated, but he understood the family was going through a lot, and there was no guarantee she'd give him anything useful as long as she was still spelled. He'd try again anyway, but next time it would be in person.

Niko spent the rest of his afternoon pouring over the documents, trying to come up with a plan for the investigation. First, he'd check out the scene of the crime, see if any clues had been left behind or if anyone who lived nearby had seen anything suspicious. He'd also make a list of Polly's closest friends and family, and he'd interview them for anything they might have to say.

But before he did any of that, he decided to search the Magical Task Force's database for any cases that might be similar. Oftentimes, criminals couldn't stop themselves from repeating the same crimes over and over again. He'd solved more than one case that way.

Settling in with a fresh mug of coffee, he got to work, searching through case file after case file. It was grueling work, but even if he'd had a team, he'd still search all the files himself. It was remarkable how sometimes just one detail could break a case wide open. If there was one in the database, he was determined to find it.

He was about halfway through his search when an old case from over a decade ago caught his eye. It was labeled as a USCC, the code for unsolved cold case. He clicked on the file and started to read.

*Victim: twenty-two-year-old female*

*Incident: Victim was compelled to rob a series of convenience stores. Shot by local security. Victim was still trying to rob the store, despite being shot in the abdomen. Witnesses testified that she seemed single-minded and robotic as she demanded the cash from the register and safe.*

*Outcome: Victim seemed to come out of the trance just before she took her last breath. Her last words were: Find Indigo Easton.*

His eyes bugged out when he spotted Indigo's name. She'd told him there was a file on her somewhere, but he intentionally hadn't looked for it. He wasn't sure why. Maybe he hadn't wanted to know. But he also knew better than most that files didn't contain the whole truth more often than not, and he wanted to hear her story from *her*.

But now he was staring down a very serious case, and this old file was more than relevant. He had no choice but to finish reading every detail in the incident report. The victim, Tricia Brighton, had robbed five convenience stores in one night, only stopping when she died from her bullet wounds.

The prime suspect had been Indigo Easton.

There were pages and pages of information on Indigo about her past, her family, and the fact that she was Tricia's roommate.

Final line of the report: *Not enough evidence. No charges filed.*

Niko sat stunned as he reread the pages again, trying to make sense of the overwhelming information. On the second round, he spotted a detail he'd missed. The victim had burn marks on her arms in the shape of daggers.

He immediately picked up his phone and called Indigo.

It went straight to voice mail. He glanced at the time, noting that all the stores on Main Street would already be closed, which meant she likely wasn't at work.

Jumping out of his chair, he grabbed his keys and headed straight for his truck. He didn't know where he'd find her, but he had to talk to her immediately. One way or another, he needed to get to the bottom of what happened a decade before with Indigo's roommate.

Once he was in his vehicle heading back to Befana Bay, he told his phone to call Braxton.

His friend picked up on the first ring. "Hey, man," Braxton said. "What are you doing right now?"

"I'm headed to Befana Bay. I'm looking for Indigo. Can you ask Lily if she has any idea where she is?"

"No need. She's here with us at the bookstore. We're working on setting up that fundraiser for the library. Why don't you stop by?"

"I'm on my way," Niko said.

Ten minutes later, Niko walked into the bookstore. The outside looked like an enchanted fairy garden with twinkling lights and spelled fireflies. Inside was full of vibrant flowers and a pleasant floral scent as if it were some sort of botanical garden instead of a musty bookstore.

Under normal circumstances, he'd have lingered and admired the work his friends had done, but tonight, he had only one thing on his mind. He hurried upstairs, following the light din of voices, and he found Lily, Brax, Mateo, Dante and Prim all standing around a display with a floating book that was being read aloud by a soothing, masculine voice that seemed to be coming from nowhere and everywhere at the same time.

"Hey," Brax said, moving over to clasp him on his back. "You made it."

"Yeah." He glanced around. "Where's Indigo?"

Brax frowned. "Sorry, brother, but she took off right

after I talked to you. She said she had something to take care of and then hurried out."

Lily glanced at him and gave him a sympathetic frown. "Don't take it personally. She just needs time."

He might be able to take that advice if he hadn't just read that old case file. But now he had a job to do. "Do you know where she is?"

"No." Prim moved to stand next to Lily and crossed her arms over her chest, looking determined. "Just let her be, Niko. She's had a rough week."

"She's not the only one," he said and then turned around and left.

When he got to the ground floor, one of the sections of books started to glow. He almost ignored them, but when he realized it was the section that Indigo had shied away from on their date, he changed course.

The first book he pulled out was titled *Exploring your Power*. The second was *Deep Dive into Harnessing Your Magic*. And the third was *Experimental Magic*. Title after title was focused on exploring magic or harnessing power. They weren't simple spell books, but rather how to become a stronger witch and create new spells and potions.

He stood there staring at the books, remembering how she'd looked when she'd pulled the first book that night.

Unsettled.

Maybe even scared.

That was not the look of a witch who was excited about tapping into her raw talents.

He made a mental note and strode out of the building.

# CHAPTER 9

THE MOMENT INDIGO heard that Niko was looking for her, she'd fled. Her flight instinct had kicked in and she'd bolted. The last few days had just been too hard. The worst thing that had ever happened in her life had come back to haunt her in a big way, and she wasn't dealing with it very well.

Memories had overwhelmed her, and she could feel herself sliding back into that dark pit of despair she'd been in for months after Tricia's death.

It wasn't a place she wanted to go again, but she knew if she didn't do something, she'd likely crawl into bed, pull up the covers, and never crawl out again.

There was only one person she wanted to talk to right then. Indigo just hoped she was home.

After leaving the bookstore, Indigo had driven back to her building. But instead of going upstairs to her apartment, she'd locked her vehicle and then set out on foot, heading to the large Victorian that sat at the foot of Main Street, overlooking the bay.

Indigo could see the lights glowing from the downstairs windows and instantly felt a little better.

She was home.

Quickening her pace, Indigo hurried to the house where she and her sisters had grown up after their mother had passed. She was half a block away when she heard the sound of raised voices carrying on the breeze.

She frowned, peering at the porch and the outline of two people. Suddenly recognition kicked in, and Indigo took off at a dead run.

"Paul!" Indigo called out from the front walkway. "Get away from my grandmother!"

Her ex turned and looked at her, his expression cold and calculating. "Why? Are you going to compel me next?"

Pure hatred of the man she'd once thought she was going to marry took over, and suddenly she was on the porch, right in his face. "What the hell are you doing here?"

"Looking for you." He sneered, making her wonder what she'd ever seen in the man.

"I don't live here," she said as if that mattered.

"I know, but you weren't at your apartment, so I tried here, figuring your grandmother could tell me where you were."

"I didn't tell him anything, Indy," Bethany Befana said, her tone haughty. "In fact, I told him to get off my property or else I'd see to it he was thrown off."

Paul ignored her. "I need you to tell me why you cursed Polly Smart."

"Who?" Indigo tried to file through her brain to see if that name was familiar, but she came up with nothing.

"Don't play stupid with me," he said, sounding impatient now as he glanced quickly at Bethany and then back to Indigo. "You know who I'm talking about. I want to know how you know her and why you put her under your spell."

"Under my spell? Are you talking about the woman who was in front of my store the other day? If so, I'd never seen her before. Now it's time for you to go. My grandmother and I have plans." The plans were a lie, but he wouldn't know that.

"Oh? Bethany said she was on her way to a coven meeting. Are you participating in those now?" His voice was dripping with judgment.

"None of your damned business." She moved past him, intending to usher her grandmother inside, but Paul caught her wrist, stopping her.

"You're not going anywhere. Not until you confess that you compelled Polly Smart."

Indigo stared down at his hand on her wrist. In a low but commanding voice, she said, "Let go, Paul."

"I don't think so." His grip tightened.

He was dressed in plain clothes, but Indigo knew he was an investigator for the state. "Are you here on official business?"

"Yes," he said.

"Then I want a lawyer," she said.

"I didn't say you're under arrest," Paul said, annoyed.

"You also won't let me go into my grandmother's house. Are you detaining me or not, Officer Pitts?"

"I want you to be honest for once. How do you know Polly Smart?" he asked again.

She ground her teeth together and yanked her wrist from his hold. "I told you that I don't know anyone named Polly. Now either arrest me or let me go. I'm tired of this game."

"Have it your way." He pulled out a pair of handcuffs and started to jamb her wrists into them, forgoing the reading of her *Miranda* rights.

"You can't arrest Indigo," Bethany spat out. "She's done nothing but refuse to have a conversation with you. Produce your arrest warrant, or I'll be raining hellfire on you, Paul."

"I don't need one," he said cheerfully. "Not when she's wanted for questioning in a murder case and she's refusing to cooperate. I can hold her for up to seventy-two hours without a warrant. I suggest you keep your cool, Bethany. I wouldn't want to have to arrest you as well."

"Call our family lawyer," Indigo said, knowing they had nothing to pin on her. She didn't even know what he was talking about.

"I'm not letting him take you," Bethany said through clenched teeth and then turned to Paul. "What is wrong with you? Indigo is a kind woman who has spent her life grieving for Tricia. And yet here you are, still convinced Indigo was responsible for what happened. Do you think your own pain is going to fade if you lock up an innocent woman?"

Tears sprang to Indigo's eyes. The gut-wrenching horror

she'd felt the day she'd learned of Tricia's death came roaring back, nearly debilitating her.

"This doesn't have to do with Tricia." Paul's voice was strained, and Indigo knew he was lying. She'd always known when he wasn't telling the truth, despite his incredible poker face. It was just a feeling born from the connection they'd once shared.

"You're a liar," she said, glaring at him.

"Shut up." He yanked on her arms, pulling her backward and then immediately pushing her toward Bethany, making her fall forward.

Pain blossomed from her kneecaps as she cried out in agony, but then Indigo quickly quieted herself. She would not give him the satisfaction.

"Get up," he ordered.

She glared up at him, not saying a word. If he was going to arrest her, she wasn't going to make it easy on him.

"What do you think you're doing?" a familiar male voice asked from the darkness just beyond the porch.

"This is official police business," Paul said with an air of superiority. "I suggest you walk away, man."

"That's not going to happen." Niko walked up the short flight of stairs and glanced down at Indigo. His expression was stormy as he reached down and gently lifted her to her feet. "Are you okay?" he asked quietly.

"As okay as I can be," she muttered.

He nodded once and then turned back to Paul.

"Just who do you think you are?" Paul demanded. "Get out of the way, or else I'll be forced to arrest you, too." He was already pulling out another set of handcuffs when Niko let out a humorless laugh.

"I wouldn't try it if I were you." Niko pulled out a badge and flashed it at the other man.

Paul's eyes narrowed as he focused on it. "Magical Task Force?"

Niko nodded. "And you just stepped right in the middle of my investigation. I suggest you release this woman before I'm forced to report you to your superiors."

"This was my case first," Paul hissed.

"That's not relevant," Niko said. "Now unlock these cuffs before I make that call."

Grumbling to himself, Paul yanked at Indigo's hands, making her grunt with pain.

"Hurt her again and you'll find out what it means to be locked in an MTF jail cell," Niko said, his voice full of steel.

"That would never stick," Paul said.

"Are you game to find out?" Niko pulled what looked like zip ties from his back pocket.

Indigo wondered briefly if he'd come to her grandmother's house to use them on her. A shiver of unease slid down her back. If Niko was investigating her, she was likely in for a rough time regardless of her innocence. Her heart sank, and she just wished a hole would open up and swallow her.

Paul quickly uncuffed Indigo and stepped back.

"There. Was that so hard?" Niko asked as he took a step, putting his body between her and Paul.

Indigo was both grateful and slightly annoyed. She had more than enough power to defend herself. The problem

THE WITCH'S LOST SPELL

was that she just couldn't because she knew that was the fastest way to get herself locked up.

"You can go now," Niko said. "And don't come back around here. This case is out of your jurisdiction."

"You mean Polly Smart's case is out of my jurisdiction," Paul said.

"I mean both." Niko crossed his arms over his wide chest. "Ms. Easton is now a vital part of the investigation, and I won't have you interfering. Understand?"

Paul glared at Niko. And then without answering, he stalked off the porch and climbed into an unmarked black SUV.

They stood there watching until the vehicle disappeared.

"Niko," Bethany said, grabbing his arm. "Thank you for showing up when you did. You saved me from doing something I probably wouldn't be proud of."

He gave Indigo's grandmother an amused smile. "I'm sort of sorry I missed that."

Indigo cleared her throat. "Can we go inside or am I headed to the Magical Task Force prison?"

"Did you commit a crime?" he asked with a cheeky grin that she didn't appreciate.

"No."

"Then it looks like you'll be sleeping in your own bed tonight."

Still annoyed, Indigo gave him a disapproving frown as she and her grandmother went back inside. To no one's surprise, Niko followed them.

# CHAPTER 10

NIKO PAUSED in Bethany's foyer and marveled at all the Wiccan artwork. He felt like he'd just stepped into an art gallery that was dedicated to the witches of Befana Bay. On one wall, there was an ornately carved broomstick that looked a lot like the ones Indigo sold in her store, only this one seemed older, more original. Along with the broomstick, there were bundles of herbs, likely hung for protection.

On the other wall, there were framed photographs of Befana Bay going back at least a hundred years. She'd chosen to showcase not only her daughter and granddaughters, but also plenty of the other residents in Befana Bay. His favorite was a black-and-white photo of a coven meeting on paddle boards. Each of the witches were dressed in a black robe and a black witch's hat. Right in the middle of the photo, there was an orca breeching the water, but none of the witches were looking at it. Instead, they all had their arms raised as if they were praying to a goddess. It was the type of photo that made him want to be a part of the community.

"This way, Mr. Morales," Bethany Befana said, slipping her arm through his to guide him into the sitting room.

Much like the foyer, the room was dedicated to all things witches. A large pentagram hung over the old fireplace mantle, and an assortment of candles and crystals and herbs were displayed on the hearth.

But the rest of the room just had comfortable looking couches and chairs along with a lovely dahlia-patterned rug.

"Your home is lovely, Bethany," he said.

"Thank you. I take great pride in this house and the history it holds," she said.

"I can see that."

"Have a seat. I'll get us some tea." Bethany gestured to the love seat, where Indigo had already perched on one end.

Her granddaughter glared at her.

Niko would have laughed if the situation hadn't been so tense already. Instead, he swallowed the impulse and took a seat next to Indigo. Before he could even open his mouth, she started the conversation for him.

"So. You read my file," she said. It was a statement. Not a question.

"Actually, no," he said, realizing he still hadn't looked her up in the database.

She let out a disbelieving huff. "You're saying you don't know anything about my past?"

"I'm not saying that," he said carefully, trying to figure out how to best navigate this conversation. The case he was working on was confidential. Technically, he wasn't supposed to discuss it with anyone except his superiors. "I got assigned a new case today," he hedged. "When I was researching it, an old case popped up that involved you. I've read that casefile, but I didn't look up whatever they've collected on you personally."

"You found Tricia's cold case," she said flatly.

"I did. Do you want to tell me about it?"

"Do I *want* to?" She snorted. "Do you want to tell me why that case is related to your current one?"

"Yes," he said honestly. "Though I'm not supposed to give specifics. I can say that the new case mirrors Tricia's in a lot of ways."

Her face paled and then she turned slightly green as she slumped back against the couch cushions. "Someone was compelled and died as a result?"

"A woman was compelled, and she almost died, but thankfully she was saved before it came to that." It was probably more than he should say, but he had a feeling he was going to need Indigo if he wanted to solve this case.

Obvious relief washed over her features. But her voice still cracked when she asked, "What happened?"

"I only have the written report so far. The victim's family refused my call, so I haven't talked to her yet. I was doing my research when I stumbled on Tricia's case. I wanted to talk to you about it first before I head out to the hospital to try again and see what I can find out from the victim."

"Is it the woman who was spelled out in front of my store?" she asked.

"No. Are you saying she was compelled?" he asked, his eyebrows raised.

She nodded.

"So we have two incidents of women being compelled within the same week," he said aloud.

Indigo suddenly sat up and met his gaze head on as she asked, "Has the spell been broken?"

"No, not that I know of."

"That's likely why she won't talk to you or anyone else. I would be surprised if she wasn't compelled to never speak about the one who spelled her." She sucked in a deep breath and let it out slowly as she added, "If you need me to help, I can break compulsion spells. It's... let's just say it's one of my gifts."

His initial reaction was to say no. Absolutely not. He'd seen what it had done to her when she'd reversed the spell on that woman in the street. It wasn't something he was eager to witness again. However, he knew that breaking compulsion spells without knowing who cast them was extremely difficult. If she could help the victim, how could he say no? "I would appreciate that."

Indigo worried the hem of her shirt as she watched her grandmother set the tea tray on the coffee table.

Bethany poured the tea and said, "There's shortbread, too. Help yourself."

Neither Niko nor Indigo indulged in the cookies, but Indigo did take one of the cups of tea.

Niko waited until she sipped her tea before saying, "I think it's your turn."

"I know. I'm just trying to summon the courage." She

gave him a weak smile. After sipping more of her tea, she said, "I created the compulsion spell."

He stared at her, speechless.

"Yeah, that's the response I expected." She pressed her lips together for a moment, closed her eyes, and said, "Tricia was my best friend. We shared an apartment and were both getting our degrees in practical magic. We did everything together, and that included our senior project."

"You created the compulsion spell for your senior project?" There was a knot in Niko's stomach as he waited for her to continue.

"Yes, but by accident. The spell was supposed to be one that stored magic in a tattoo." She rubbed at her forearm, and he noticed that the tattoo that had shown up when she helped that woman outside of her shop was now gone again. "Then once the magic was concentrated in the tattoo, I could call on it for spells without having to do incantations or involved coven circles or herb offerings. You know, speed up the process. I imagined using the magic mostly for chores or as a third hand when my hands were full. You know, practical stuff."

"I gather it didn't go as planned," he said.

"Not at all. Tricia and I did the spell together because we needed combined power to cast it. We thought it worked, but when I tried to call on the magic in my tattoo to clean the fireplace, the magic actually compelled Tricia to do it. She was in a scary trance, and I immediately reversed the spell. It knocked me out for two days."

"It even drained her tattoos of the magic," Bethany said

softly from where she was perched on the edge of an armchair.

"I noticed they seem to come and go," Niko said.

Indigo drained the rest of her tea and put the cup down. "They faded after I reversed the spell that day with Tricia. They came back for the first time the other day when I helped that woman." She glanced down at her tattoo-free arms. "They faded again not long after that."

"So an echo of the spell is still with you?" Niko guessed.

"Maybe." She shrugged. "I really don't know. After we realized we'd cast a compulsion spell, we trashed the experiment and never tried again."

"Befana witches don't mess around with illegal magic," Bethany said with a sniff.

"At least not knowingly." Indigo looked a little dejected as she slumped back into the chair.

Niko knew he should be skeptical of that claim. No witch he'd ever known would admit to using forbidden magic. At least not the ones who hadn't already dove head-first into dark magic. But still, he believed Indigo. She gave off an air of honesty that he couldn't ignore. "So what happened after that? What happened to Tricia?"

Indigo's eyes misted with tears, but she quickly blinked them back. "I don't actually know what happened with Tricia. You probably know more than I do if you were able to read her case file. After we realized we'd created an illegal spell, we told our faculty adviser what happened with our attempt and asked for more time to create something else. He granted us a few more weeks."

"Was Tricia on board with burying the compulsion spell?" Niko asked, trying to get a read on what went wrong.

"What? Of course, she was. We both agreed that it was a spell that should never see the light of day again." Indigo glanced at her grandmother and then grimaced.

"What was that look for?" he asked.

Bethany was still looking at her granddaughter when she said, "I have always thought that Tricia decided to revisit that spell and that's how she ended up cursed. I just don't know who else was involved. It takes two to tango with that one."

"Tricia wouldn't have done that," Indigo insisted. "I knew her better than anyone... besides Paul."

"Paul? The a-hole who tried to arrest you?" Niko was still annoyed by the state investigator.

"Yes, he was her brother," Indigo said with a sigh. "Well, half brother. They have different dads, but they were both raised by their mom. With no fathers in the picture, they were pretty close."

"And he was Indigo's fiancé," Bethany offered.

"Grandma!" Indigo stood, staring down at the matriarch.

"I know you don't like thinking about it, honey, but if Niko is going to be able to help, he should have all the facts," she said calmly.

"Your ex-fiancé was trying to arrest you?" Niko asked and immediately regretted it when Indigo's features hardened. "Sorry. Seems like he's holding onto a serious grudge."

Indigo let out a humorless laugh. "You could say that. He

blames me for Tricia's death. Needless to say, we don't really care for each other these days."

"He blames you because you two created the spell together?" Niko asked.

"No, he thinks I spelled her and that's why I was investigated," she said with a deep sadness in her tone. "And why I was asked to leave school before I graduated."

He sat with that for a second before responding. "I know you were never arrested. Why?"

She huffed out a laugh. "Airtight alibi. The day Tricia was spelled, I was asked to cover for the manager at the yoga studio where I worked. It was my normal day off, but I was there from morning until nearly 11:00 p.m. that night. I had dozens of eyewitnesses come forward to confirm I was there, so they really had nothing to go on."

"And still Paul thinks our Indigo had something to do with it," Bethany said with a sneer of disgust. "He turned out to be a giant disappointment."

"That's an understatement," Indigo said softly. "And now he's back trying to blame me for this curse. The irony is that I stay away from any and all experimental magic now. I spend my day doing simple charms on my brooms and leave everything else to the rest of the witches of Befana Bay."

Niko felt a ball of rage form in his gut as he mulled over everything Indigo had said. He wanted to jump up off the love seat, go find Paul, and start rearranging his body parts. Conducting an investigation was one thing, but ignoring evidence in favor of a half-baked theory was despicable. A good investigator had to go where the clues took them, not try to twist the clues to fit a narrative. He clenched his fists when he thought of a childhood friend named Casey. She hadn't deserved to be targeted either. But because she had no one to stand up for her, she'd died in a Magical Task Force prison before he'd found a way to prove her innocence.

He turned his attention to Indigo. "If Paul comes around you again for any reason, I want you to call me ASAP. Understand?"

"Thank you, Niko," she said kindly. "But I don't need a babysitter. I can take care of myself."

"I'm sure you can," he said with a nod. "However, humor me. We can all use a little help every now and again." Niko stood and rocked back on his heels. "I should go."

Indigo stared at her feet and then looked up and said, "Thank you for believing in me."

He brushed a lock of hair behind her ear and smiled down at her. "Always."

They both walked out onto Bethany's porch. And when Indigo indicated she'd be walking home, Niko said, "Not without me."

Her jaw tensed and he was sure she was going to argue, but as she glanced down the darkened street, she let out a breath and said, "Fine. But don't get any ideas."

Oh, he had ideas, but he pushed them aside as he gave Indigo a friendly smile and happily escorted her home.

# CHAPTER 11

INDIGO FELT LIGHTER than she had in days. It seemed purging her soul to Niko had lifted some sort of weight off her shoulders. She glanced at him as they walked the few blocks down to her building. When was the last time she'd felt safe with any man? Not physically safe, but mentally and emotionally.

Maybe she was being too hopeful. Or too trusting. But she wasn't trusting by nature. Not these days. So the fact that he'd found a way to earn her trust was remarkable.

Niko slowed and then suddenly paused. "Is that Paul standing in front of your building?"

Indigo squinted through the darkness and made out the familiar shape. "Dammit," she muttered. "I thought he'd go away after that confrontation."

"It appears Mr. Eager is dying for a can of whoop-ass." Niko took off, doubling his pace.

Indigo hurried to catch up with him.

Paul must have heard their footsteps, because he turned in their direction, and when he spotted Niko, he also cursed and then hurried to the black SUV that was parked across the street.

"Has he ever bothered you here before?" Niko asked.

She shook her head. "I haven't spoken to him since the day I was told I was no longer a suspect in Tricia's case."

"I bet that didn't go well."

"Not at all." Indigo crossed her arms over her chest as the memory came flooding back. "In fact, I would have called the police station to get him removed, but since he worked there, I knew his buddies would only cover for him."

Niko's eyes darkened and he nearly growled when he asked, "Did that asshole hurt you?"

"Physically? No." She grimaced. "But he sure did try to dump a mountain of grief and guilt on me."

He wrapped an arm around her shoulders and pulled her in for a side hug.

Indigo knew she should probably pull away. This man had already found ways around her barriers, and giving in to the physical comfort he was offering would only make it that much harder to stick to her resolve not to date law enforcement.

A small voice in the back of her mind wondered, *if you trust him, why are you keeping him at arm's length?*

She steeled herself against the intruding thoughts. There was no question why she had to keep her distance. He was law enforcement. What if he suddenly decided he didn't believe her? She'd be quite literally sleeping in the lion's den.

And while the idea of having someone in a position of authority who was on her side was really appealing, she just didn't think she could let her guard down enough to go there.

"I don't want to leave until I'm sure that jerk isn't coming back tonight," Niko said. "How do you feel about dinner? We could head to The Salt Circle, or if you prefer, we could stay in and make some pasta."

What was that about not stepping into the lion's den? Indigo was already nodding before she could think anything through. "Let's just stay in. I'm not really up for going out." She gave him a sheepish smile. "But we might have to scrounge for ingredients. I'm not sure when I last went to the store."

"A challenge!" he said, looking far too pleased. "I'm ready. Lead the way."

Indigo did just that as she headed up the stairs to her apartment.

The first thing she did once they were inside was find a bottle of wine. "Is red okay?"

"Obviously," he said, already opening her refrigerator to inspect the ingredients.

"Good, because I'm out of white." She found a couple of wine glasses and got busy pouring. By the time she handed him a glass, he already had a pile of ingredients on the counter.

She inventoried his haul, surprised to see that he'd found

a handful of vegetables and what looked to be a block of parmesan cheese.

"Do you have pasta and marinara sauce or olive oil?" he asked.

"No marinara, but I do have olive oil, and it would be a cold day in hell before you'd find this apartment without a stash of pasta."

"Excellent. It looks like we have the makings for pasta primavera," he said, opening her cabinets to look for the pasta.

Indigo went into the small pantry just off the kitchen and returned with some penne pasta and a bottle of olive oil. "Need anything else?"

"Nope. Not unless you've got some sourdough in that closet."

She wrinkled her nose. "Sorry. Your luck has run out."

"Damn. Oh well. We'll just have to make do." He gestured to her bar-top counter and said, "Have a seat. I've got this."

"I can help," she insisted, eyeing the vegetables. "Put me in the game, coach. I can chop with the best of them."

He chuckled softly. "Okay. Sure." He handed her a yellow squash and said, "Do your worst."

Before grabbing her cutting board and a knife, Indigo synced her phone up with her Bluetooth speaker and then chose her favorite playlist.

When "Witchy Woman" by the Eagles came on, Niko eyed her and said, "Appropriate choice."

She winked. "My grandmother might have had a bit of influence over my musical education."

"Remind me to thank Bethany for her cool musical tastes."

For the next thirty minutes, they worked together to get dinner ready, and by the time Niko put their plates on her table, Indigo was practically drooling.

"It smells fantastic," Indigo said as she refilled their wine glasses. "Who knew I had anything of nutritional value in my kitchen?"

He took a seat and then lifted his glass for a toast. "To good old-fashioned home cooking with friends."

Indigo was tingling with happiness as she touched her glass to his. "To home cooking and friends."

Niko held her gaze while he took another sip of wine, and Indigo felt a spark of attraction that caused gooseflesh to pop out over her skin. If it wasn't for the fact that she was so hungry, she might have been tempted to forgo dinner altogether and just haul him into her bedroom. Her cheeks heated at the image, and she vaguely wondered what had happened to her convictions.

Her eyes locked on the wine glass, making her chuckle. *Oh, that's what happened.*

"Care to share the joke?" Niko asked her.

She quickly shook her head. "It's nothing. I was just laughing at myself."

He raised one eyebrow, waiting.

She waved a hand, indicating she wasn't going to elaborate, and then changed the subject as she asked, "How did you end up working at the Magical Task Force? You must have been in mundane law enforcement before that, right?"

He didn't say anything at first.

"I'm sorry, is that something you're not allowed to talk about?" she asked, feeling foolish. Less than an hour ago, she just gotten done pouring out all of her secrets, and now he seemed to be clamming up over a seemingly simple question.

"No, no. Nothing like that," he said and then took another long pause. "There's a reason I'm here other than I just like your company."

She glanced at the bedroom and then back at him with her eyebrows raised.

He laughed, his eyes twinkling with mirth. "I'm not going to deny that I definitely am interested in... that. After our night back in Florida, it would be disingenuous to say otherwise." He let his gaze roam up and down her torso and then back up, where he met her eyes again. "But that's not what I was talking about." All the humor left his expression when he added, "I've had my own run-ins with the law. Run-ins that left me very distrustful of certain law officers."

Indigo leaned forward, and with her elbow on the table, she rested her chin on her palm. "Do you have a file, too, Niko Morales? How did you ever get them to give you a badge?"

His soft chuckle was back, but he sobered quickly. "No. I was never accused of anything. But my best friend was. She was my next door neighbor, and we pretty much grew up together. Our moms helped each other out, and it seemed like Casey and I were at each other's houses nearly every day."

He rubbed at his brow, and she wondered if he was getting a headache.

But when he looked up at her again, there was a fire in his eyes that almost made her want to jerk back.

"Casey was accused of putting a death spell on the old man who lived across the street from us," he said, his tone full of fury.

Indigo's chest tightened as she forced out, "A death spell?"

"Yes. The man was an angry soul who tormented all the kids on the street by letting his German shepherd loose to chase them all over the place. He was one of those creepers who everyone stayed away from. No one trusted him. Casey wasn't afraid of him and just never paid him any attention. She'd say he was a weak, lonely man who was only looking for attention."

"She was probably right," Indigo said. "He sure sounds like the type."

"Maybe." He shrugged. "Anyway, he pissed off the wrong person, and someone cursed him. They found out when he went to the hospital with heart failure. It was quickly learned that a spell caused it. He accused Casey, said that he saw her working dark magic in her garage. The next thing I knew, she was arrested and taken by the Magical Task Force."

"She didn't do it, did she?" There was no doubt in Indigo's mind that his friend had been innocent. His anger was too palpable.

"No. But circumstantial evidence was found in her

garage that tied her to the spell." He sighed heavily. "She was quickly convicted despite there being no actual proof, and she was incarcerated for nearly a year while I worked to find out who cursed him. By the time I figured it out, it was too late."

"Too late?" Indigo pressed her hand to her heart, fearing the worst.

"Too late to preserve any of her innocence." A muscle in his jaw pulsed. "When she came out, she was radicalized and went deep into forbidden magic." He closed his eyes for a long moment. "Nothing I said or did could pull her out of it."

"What happened?"

His expression was blank when he said, "She passed away three years after she was released. One of the dark spells backfired, and that was the end."

Indigo was speechless. That could have been her if she hadn't had an airtight alibi all those years ago. She liked to think that she wouldn't have succumbed to the dark side, but how could she know what she'd be like if she was locked up in a paranormal prison for a year?

"I'm so sorry, Niko. So you entered law enforcement because of Casey?"

He nodded. "I wanted to clean up the agency from the inside. Be the agent that Casey deserved the first time she was accused. I'm not saying she didn't bear responsibility for how she lived her life after she was freed, but there's no doubt that her incarceration was the catalyst for that lifestyle. I want to bring down bad actors while also making sure that innocents aren't accused just so some power-starved, ego-driven jackass can further his career."

Indigo reached across the table and slipped her fingers through his. "That's very noble."

"It's not noble. It's just… decency." He grimaced. "Sorry. I didn't mean to get on my soapbox. Anyway, I wasn't a police officer before I joined the MTF. After I helped exonerate Casey, I was sort of taken under the wing of the division chief and got my foot in the door that way."

Indigo drained the last of her wine and said, "I'm glad you did. The world needs good people to serve."

"Unlike *Paul*," he said. "That guy is exactly the kind of investigator who is not above bending the rules to get the outcome he needs. But don't worry. He'll have to go through me first."

Indigo couldn't help but smile at him. "Are you going to be my bodyguard or something?"

"Or something." He stood and started to gather their empty plates.

"Oh no. The chef does not do dishes." Indigo waved him toward the couch. "Let me. And then we'll have gelato."

"You have gelato?" he asked, looking hopeful.

"Yep. Any self-respecting Italian girl wouldn't be caught dead without some in her freezer." She took the plates from him, kissed his cheek, and then got to work.

Once the kitchen was sparkling clean, she grabbed the jar of gelato and two spoons before joining him on the couch.

He took his spoon and dipped out a bit of chocolate gelato, but instead of tasting it himself, he held it out to her.

Indigo kept her gaze locked with Niko's as she closed her lips around the spoon.

His gaze heated, and suddenly everything that had happened that night hit Indigo like a ton of bricks. He'd stepped in and saved her from being arrested. He'd listened to everything she had to say about the circumstances around Tricia's death, and not only had he not judged her, but he'd also been sympathetic. Then he'd made her dinner and shared a deeply personal story about his childhood friend.

She felt closer to him than she'd ever felt with anyone else outside her immediate family.

All of her reasons for staying away from him fled and just like that, she no longer cared about her self-imposed rules.

"Niko?"

His voice was husky when he said, "Yes?"

"Will you stay the night... with me?"

His lips twitched into the sexiest half smile as he gave her the tiniest of nods.

She stood, took the gelato back to the freezer, and then returned and held her hand out to him.

The warmth of his hand on hers sent tingles of anticipation over her skin, and when they were in her bedroom, she slowly unbuttoned her blouse. As she let it fall to the floor, Niko was there, wrapping her in his arms.

His warm breath tickled her skin as he asked, "Are you sure about this?"

"Absolutely," she said, her gaze fixated on his lips. "Now kiss me."

"Gladly." His lips claimed hers and the rest of the world faded away as she finally gave herself over to the man she'd been dreaming about ever since she'd walked away from him after that one perfect night down in Florida.

# CHAPTER 12

NIKO WOKE ONCE AGAIN with the woman of his dreams in his arms. Only this time, her warm, naked body was pressed against his, and when he gently ran his fingers over her golden skin, she let out a small moan of pleasure.

He knew if he had his way, he'd stay right there, exploring every inch of her body over and over and over again. Unfortunately he'd gotten a text that Polly Smart was being released from the hospital that afternoon, and her parents were taking her to their home in Arizona for the time being. If he wanted to interview her, it was now or never.

"Hmm, what a way to wake up," Indigo said as she turned over to face him.

He bent his head and brushed his lips over hers. "I'd stay here all day if I could."

"It's my day off. There's nothing stopping me from doing just that," she said as she teased her fingers over his pecs.

He quickly grabbed her hand, stopping her.

Her eyebrows shot up. "Something wrong?"

"The only thing wrong is that I don't have time to show you just how insatiable I can be." He let go of her and quickly rolled out of the bed before his willpower lost the battle against his desire for her. "We've got to get to the hospital to interview the victim in my case."

The sweet but sexy vibe Indigo had been giving off suddenly vanished as she sat up, pulling the sheet up to cover herself. "We? You really want me to go with you?"

"You did say you could break the spell if she's still compelled, didn't you?" he asked.

"Yeah."

He smiled down at her, feeling triumphant as he held out his hand. "Good. Let's shower so we can catch her before she's discharged."

She let him tug her from the bed and into the en suite bathroom.

As she turned the water on in the shower, she eyed him, letting her gaze wander the length of his naked body. "You're pretty pleased with yourself, aren't you?"

He nodded as he tugged her into the shower.

An hour later, smiling like two teenagers, they walked out of her apartment together and down to the café for coffee and pastries.

"Not exactly a breakfast of champions," Indigo said and then took another bite of her coffee cake.

"I think we burned enough calories last night to justify a serving of pastry," he said with a wink.

Her face flushed, and he decided she'd never looked sexier.

When they were finished with their pastries, Niko took her hand in his and led her to his Ram truck.

"Is this how you treat all your partners?" she asked with an amused glint in her eye as he held the door open for her.

"No, but that's mostly because my only other partner's name was Bud, and he wasn't nearly as good-looking as you."

She laughed and climbed in.

For the next forty minutes, they bantered all the way to the hospital. It wasn't until he parked and they got out of the truck that Indigo sobered. He got the impression that she was happy to be distracted so that she didn't have to think too much about why she had been asked to tag along. He knew everything about his case was bringing up memories she'd rather not revisit.

"I appreciate the hell out of you for doing this," he said.

She nodded once and stared straight ahead as they made their way inside.

He was all business when they reached Polly's room. He knocked twice and waited until a woman came out to greet them.

"Mrs. Smart? I'm Agent Morales from the Magical Task Force. I was really hoping I could have a minute with Polly before you take her back to Arizona."

The woman glanced over her shoulder into the room before she stepped all the way out and closed the door behind her. "My husband won't like it."

Niko nodded. "I understand, but I really am here to help. Neither of us want to do anything to upset Polly."

The woman glanced at Indigo briefly before turning her attention back to Niko. "Listen, I want to find out who did this to her more than anything, but she's not…" She shook her head. "Polly can't really answer questions right now. She's just not totally there. The trauma—"

"Mrs. Smart," Indigo interjected. "I've had some experience with compulsions spells. I think I might be able to help her. If you'll allow it, I'd like to meet her and see if my gifts can free her from the lingering effect of the spell."

Hope shone in the mother's eyes, but she quickly glanced back at the door again and bit down on her bottom lip.

"I'm happy to speak to your husband if you'd like," Indigo said, her tone full of compassion.

"No." Mrs. Smart shook her head with conviction. "If you think you can help my Polly, then it's worth a shot."

Relief washed over Indigo's face, and Niko felt a sense of pride as he watched her. She was full of compassion and determination. Her empathy for Polly's mother was undeniable. And that was exactly what was missing with most MTF agents.

Polly's mother opened the door and led them into the room. A thin man with salt-and-pepper hair sat at the bedside of the red-headed young woman who was dressed and staring blankly at the wall.

Indigo sucked in a sharp breath.

"Who are you?" the man asked as he stood.

"This is Agent Morales from the Magical Task Force and..." Mrs. Smart looked at Indigo expectantly.

"This is Indigo Easton," Niko said. "She's well versed in compulsion spells and is here to see if she can help."

The man eyed them both suspiciously. "My daughter is in no condition to talk to anyone."

Niko opened his mouth to speak, but Indigo beat him to it and said, "I think I can help with that. I've reversed compulsion spells before, and I'd be happy to try again... if you're agreeable."

The man looked like he was ready to refuse, but Mrs. Smart stepped in and said, "If they can help our baby, then I'm willing to let them try."

Polly continued to stare straight ahead as if no one was even in the room.

"If you think that's the right thing to do, Dana, then okay," the man relented as he stepped back.

Niko followed Indigo to the side of the bed. He introduced himself and Indigo and then asked, "Polly, do you know how you got here to the hospital?"

"An ambulance," she said.

"Do you know what happened to you that caused your hospital stay?"

"There was a fire. I suffered smoke inhalation, dehydration, and a few minor burns." Her answers were all monotone, robot-like. He had to admit that it was unnerving.

Indigo motioned that she wanted to talk to the woman, and Niko backed off.

"Polly, do you remember participating in any spells before you blacked out?"

The woman didn't answer.

"Okay, do you mind if I hold your hands?"

Still no answer.

"Do whatever you have to do," Dana Smart whispered as her voice cracked.

Niko moved a little closer to Indigo just in case she needed any help. He instinctively reached into his pocket and wrapped his fingers around the crystal he carried there. It was a protection crystal, meant to neutralize any spell that he might be hit with. He didn't expect either one of them to attack him with a spell, but magic was unpredictable and he preferred to be prepared.

But he should have known he wouldn't need it. He just watched in awe as Indigo held onto Polly's hands, recited her incantation, and then unleashed her blue ice magic.

Immediately two daggers appeared on Polly's forearms, but as the blue ice magic retreated and the daggers lit with flames, Mrs. Smart let out a cry of alarm.

Niko spun around and held his hands up. "It'll be okay. I promise."

A moment later, Indigo let out a cry as her own arms lit with the fire in the shape of the daggers. She stumbled backward and fell to the tiled floor, her face white and the flames gone, leaving only the dagger tattoos in their place.

"Indigo," he said softly. "You're okay." He looked up to see Polly glancing around the room in confusion. There was no trace of the fire or the daggers on her arms.

"Mom?" Polly said in a small voice.

Dana let out a cry of relief and then rushed to her daughter's side, nearly crushing her with a hug. Her father joined them, and the three of them were locked in a hug, both parents crying.

Niko picked Indigo up into his arms and carried her out of the room. When one of the nurses saw them, she rushed over and immediately directed them into an empty room. She got busy taking Indigo's vitals while barking orders to another nurse.

The entire time, Niko sat next to her, holding her hand, knowing that all she needed was one of her grandmother's restoring potions and some rest.

Indigo blinked at him, and with a hoarse voice she said, "Go get your interview."

"I'm not leaving you after that," he insisted.

"You have to," she said weakly. "Go."

Niko hesitated, but when she mouthed *Go* again, he got up and strode to the other room.

He found the Smarts all sitting together, both of her parents talking at once while Polly stared at them, confusion all over her face. It wasn't the blank expression she'd worn before. This was pure bafflement.

He cleared his throat.

The Smarts stopped talking and looked at him.

Dana Smart ran over and tackle-hugged him. "You saved our girl."

"Actually, Indigo did that. I know she'll be pleased to hear that Polly is doing better."

"I'd like to thank her myself," Dana said.

"Me, too," Mr. Smart added.

He nodded, understanding that they wanted to express their gratitude. "She's next door, but she's pretty wiped out. I'm sure she wouldn't mind seeing you for a minute, but just keep it short. Using that kind of magic is really taxing."

"Of course." The two elder Smarts hurried out of the room, leaving Niko alone with Polly.

"Hello," he said.

"Hi." She raised her hand tentatively.

He walked over to the side of the bed and held his hand out to her. "I'm Agent Morales with the Magical Task Force, and I'm investigating your case. I'm hoping you can answer a few questions for me."

The young woman visibly gulped but gave him a small nod.

He checked the notes on his phone. "You're a student at Olympic Witches University, right?"

Polly pushed back a fallen lock of her red hair and nodded.

"Do you remember how you ended up at that burning house?"

She shook her head. "I don't remember anything about it to be honest. I can see the inside of the house, but what I did there or why I was there is fuzzy."

"Was anyone else there?" he asked.

"I don't..." Her brow furrowed. "You know, I think there was someone, but I can't see who or anything." She let out a tiny growl of irritation. "It's like the memory is right there, but I can't access it."

That was likely a memory spell, but since some of them could be permanent, he didn't say anything. He didn't want

THE WITCH'S LOST SPELL

to cause her any more stress. "How about you just tell me the last thing you remember before you found yourself in that house?"

She thought for a long moment and then looked up and said, "I was working with my professor on my senior project."

Unease settled in Niko's gut. "Your professor? Which one?"

"Professor Cannon. She was helping me develop a potion that would replace eyeglasses. Can you imagine? No contacts. No glasses. To me it seems like a miracle."

"That would be helpful," he agreed as he wrote down the information in his notes. "Can you tell me your overall feelings about Professor Cannon?"

"What do you mean? Do you want to know if I like her?"

"Sure. Or if you ever had an off feeling or vibe about her," he prompted. He was starting to wonder if maybe this Professor Cannon was the one who'd decided to compel both Tricia and Polly. So far the only thing the two cases seemed to have in common besides the spell itself was that the students were working on their final projects.

"No off vibe at all!" Polly said, shaking her head forcefully. "Professor Cannon is my favorite teacher at that school. The only vibe she gives is a cool witchy one."

"Do you have any idea who might want to compel you and force you to... Well, compel you to do anything against your will?" he asked.

Polly picked at her fingernails nervously and then gave her head a violent shake. "I feel like I *should* know something. But I just don't. How can that be?" she asked him earnestly.

"I don't know, Polly. It could be trauma. You know, your psyche protecting you from something. Or it could be magical. Some sort of temporary memory loss. It's hard to say." He pulled out a business card. "If you remember anything else, will you call me?"

"Yes." She nodded. "And please tell your friend thank you. I knew I was trapped, but I had no way to get out. She saved me."

Niko squeezed her hand. "I'll tell her."

The Smarts returned just as Niko was leaving. He nodded at them and went to find Indigo.

# CHAPTER 13

"You look tired," Kinsley said as she flipped her long brown hair over her shoulder. "Did you overdo the fun yesterday?" She leaned over the front counter and pumped her eyebrows up and down as if insinuating something.

They'd just opened Brooms that Vroom, and Indigo felt barely functional. She refrained from rolling her eyes, but that was probably because she was too weak to move them. After the visit to the hospital, Niko had brought her back to her apartment and then stayed with her while she slept for nearly eighteen hours. At some point while she was dead to the world, he'd secured one of her grandmother's potions, clearly because the man was a saint. She'd downed the potion when she'd woken up, and while it had done the trick to clear some of the cobwebs, she still wasn't feeling a hundred percent.

"I knew I was barking up the wrong tree with that one,

but with a man that good-looking, it's not like I couldn't try," Kinsley said. "Amiright?"

"I'm sorry, what?" Indigo asked, having no idea what she was talking about.

"Niko. Hello. I saw you two leave your apartment yesterday, looking mighty cozy, too. And his truck is still parked right outside as well." She tsked. "Were you trying to hide the fact that you two have something going on? Because if you are, you're doing a pretty bad job of it."

"I'm not..." Indigo shook her head at her employee. "I'm not sure this is appropriate work conversation."

"Oh." Kinsley looked defeated as she straightened and took a step back. "I'm so sorry. I'll—"

Indigo held her hand up. "Stop. Never mind. I'm just really out of it today. Niko and I... I don't know what to say about us other than he's been helping me with something." More like a few things, one of which was protecting her from a vengeful ex while sharing her bed. But Kinsley didn't need to know any of those details. "We're... friends."

"Really?" Kinsley let out a soft chuckle when Niko walked in carrying a coffee tray, a pastry bag, and a single rose. When Kinsley spoke again, her voice was dripping with sarcasm. "Definitely looks like friends."

A huge smile claimed Indigo's lips when Niko handed her the rose. "You know you're not being the least bit subtle. Kinsley over here was just grilling me about you."

He barely glanced at the other woman as he shrugged one shoulder. "There's nothing to hide as far as I'm concerned."

She wanted to ask if she was a conflict of interest with

the case he was working on, but she didn't want to say anything about that in front of Kinsley. So she just said, "Right. Niko and I are just friends."

"Friends who spend the night," Kinsley muttered as the bell on the door buzzed and she slipped out from behind the counter to help the customer.

Indigo pulled him aside. "Aren't you worried that your boss might think it's a conflict of interest to date me when you're working on your new case?"

"Why? You're not involved in this new case at all," he said. "Sure, you have information that's proving to be important, but you are neither a victim nor a suspect. In the eyes of the MTF policies, we're nowhere near breaking any sort of protocol."

"Good." Indigo leaned into him, enjoying the warmth of his skin after being in air conditioning all morning. "Because I think I'm starting to like having you around."

His slow, easy smile made her want to drag him back upstairs, but that would have to wait until after the store closed.

"What's on your agenda today?" she asked him.

"I'm going to do more research on my case. I actually want to head to Olympic Witches University and conduct a couple of interviews there."

Hearing the name of her former college, the one she'd failed to graduate from, made her stomach churn with nerves. After she'd left—no, after they made her leave—she hadn't stepped foot on the campus since. It wasn't just that they didn't believe her when she said she had nothing to do with Tricia's compulsion, it was also the university itself.

Thinking about her time there, and ultimately how Tricia's time was cut short, just hurt too much.

"In fact," Niko continued. "I was hoping you could come with me. I need to interview some of the faculty about the compulsion spells happening right under their noses."

Indigo felt her insides go cold. "I can't go back there."

"The last thing I want is to cause you more stress, but if you change your mind," he said, empathy practically radiating off him, "I'll head out late this afternoon."

"I won't," she said. But even as the words flew out of her mouth, she wasn't so sure. Maybe, just maybe it was time to face her demons. She started to call Niko back, but he was already out the door and climbing into his truck. It was just as well. It'd give her time to think and mull over Niko's request.

"INDIGO? CAN I TAKE A BREAK?" Kinsley asked as she practically hung off the customer she'd been helping. Only when Indigo looked closer, the man wasn't a customer at all. He was Mateo, Dante's brother, and he looked completely smitten with Kinsley from the way he was gazing at her. Moon-eyed and everything. "Mateo here is dying to buy me a meal." She batted her eyelashes at the poor bookseller.

Indigo wondered what spell Kinsley had put on him and then quickly shook her head. Kinsley didn't need a spell. She was a gorgeous twenty-two-year-old who flirted with the best of them. It was obvious what Mateo wanted.

Chuckling to herself, she waved them off and told them

to take their time. Alone time in the shop was exactly what she needed.

INDIGO GLANCED at the clock again and scowled. Kinsley had gone to lunch with Mateo over four hours ago and had never returned. She hadn't answered any of Indigo's texts either. She knew she'd told Kinsley to take her time, but four hours and no communication? That was something else entirely. Frustrated, she walked into the back of the store, where she found Luke, her assistant, reorganizing for a shipment they were due to receive in a few days.

"Hey, boss," Luke said, leaning against a supply rack. His handsome face was red from exertion, and he'd sweat right through his Brooms that Vroom T-shirt. "What's up?"

"You've been working hard," she said, reaching into a mini fridge and pulling out a bottle of water for him.

"It's all in a good day's work." He took the water and gave her a grateful smile. He'd always been single-minded when he was on a task, forgetting to hydrate and take breaks.

"Kinsley never came back from lunch, and something unexpected came up this afternoon that I have to take care of. Have you gotten to a point where you can stop organizing for today?"

"Sure," he said after taking a long swig of water. "Give me a few minutes to clean up, and then I'll take over the store."

She gave Luke a grateful smile. "Thanks. You're a lifesaver."

He gave her a small shrug. "Just doing my job."

Indigo had lucked out when Luke had come to work with her. He had come to Befana Bay to be a production assistant on a movie that was being filmed there but had fallen in love with the magical bayside town and decided to stay. The day he'd walked into her broom shop had changed both of their lives. She finally had someone she could count on, and he'd found a stable job where he was appreciated that afforded him the life he wanted.

Fifteen minutes later, Luke appeared from the back room, freshly washed up and in a clean Brooms that Vroom T-shirt. His brow creased with concern when he asked, "Have you heard from Kinsley yet?"

Indigo shook her head. "Not a word."

"I hope everything's okay." Luke pulled out his phone and sent a text. "I know you already tried to reach her, but it's worth a shot."

"I did. I also texted Niko for Mateo's number. I'll call him as soon as Niko replies." Indigo didn't know Kinsley all that well, but she didn't think she was the type to just run out on a job without notice. And she was getting more and more worried by the minute.

Luke stared at his phone for a few beats and said, "Text sent. I'll let you know if I hear from her."

"Thanks, Luke." Indigo gave him a grateful smile. "I've got to get going. It's highly unlikely I'll be back before closing time. Just let me know if you hear from Kinsley, and I'll do the same, okay?"

He gave her a small salute. "You got it, boss. See you tomorrow?"

She shook her head. "It's my day off. Kinsley was supposed to be here to help you. Hopefully that's still the case, but if not, call me if you need help. I'll come in."

He frowned at her. "I can handle it."

"I'm sure you can, but this time of year you just never know how busy it might be," she said, squeezing his arm as she walked by. "I don't want to take my favorite employee for granted."

He chuckled softly. "I doubt there's any chance of that. Have a good afternoon and don't worry about a thing here. I've got it under control."

She nodded at him, knowing that was true. Then she hurried upstairs to grab a quick bite to eat and freshen up before Niko was supposed to pick her up. As she was walking into her apartment, her phone pinged with a message from Niko. He relayed Mateo's number and indicated he'd be there in ten minutes.

Indigo immediately called Mateo but was greeted with voice mail. "Damn," she muttered and then left a message. "Hi, Mateo, I'm wondering if Kinsley is still with you. If so, could you have her give me a call? If not, could you let me know when you parted ways? I was expecting her back at the shop today, and I'm just getting a little worried. Thanks."

Frustrated and also a little annoyed at the thought that Kinsley could have just blown her off, she dropped the phone into her purse and went to freshen up. By the time she made it back downstairs, Niko was already waiting at the curb.

"Hi." She smiled at him as she climbed into his truck.

"Hi." He pumped his eyebrows at her, looking a little ridiculous.

"If that's your form of flirting, you might want to work on it," she teased.

"I'm saving my best moves for later," he said as he pulled out onto Main Street.

Shaking her head, Indigo chuckled. "I can hardly wait." There was humor in her tone, but as soon as the words faded away, reality started to kick in. The entire purpose of their trip was to head to Olympic Witches University, a place she thought she'd never visit again. Not in this lifetime anyway.

"Are you okay?" Niko asked, obviously sensing her mood change.

"Honestly, I don't know." She glanced over at him. "I've spent a lot of the last ten years pretending that those four years I spent at OWU never happened. And now... Well, I guess there's no running from the past after all."

His grip tightened on the steering wheel, and she kept her gaze focused on his white knuckles as he spoke. "I can only imagine how hard this is for you, but I hope you know that I wouldn't have asked if I didn't think it was vital to have your input."

"I'm not sure if I'll be able to offer anything, but if I can somehow help you figure out who spelled Polly, then I'll do whatever it takes... even if it means facing down my demons." She gave him a weak smile. The truth was, as apprehensive as Indigo was to be going back to the place that had nearly broken her, she knew it was something she had to do. If not for Polly, then for herself. If one more person was harmed by the spell that she created while she did nothing to stop it, she'd never forgive herself.

Niko glanced at her. "I'd bet a month's paycheck that you don't need me, but I'll be right by your side anyway for whatever you need today."

"Thanks, but don't take that bet. You didn't know me back then, and I'm afraid the minute I step on campus I'll revert right back to being that scared young woman." She couldn't believe she was being so honest with him, or herself for that matter. But somehow, acknowledging her fears was giving her the strength she needed to face her past.

"The minute it's too much for you, I'll get you out of there," Niko promised.

Indigo nodded once, knowing that she wouldn't do anything that would hurt his investigation, even if it meant enduring whatever was waiting for her on campus.

When the truck rolled up to the front gates of the prestigious school, Indigo's head swam as her pulse quickened with unease. At the same time, she admired the beautifully manicured grounds and the blooming dahlias that framed the entrance. The place had always been so inviting. So warm. And she'd always felt at peace there. Or at least she had until everything had gone to crap and she'd been banned from her happy place.

She stared out the window, taking in the large trees that shaded the campus. Students lounged on the lawn, using backpacks as pillows, or sat against tree trunks as they studied. It all seemed so... normal. As if nothing nefarious had ever happened or would ever happen there.

Indigo knew better.

"The experimental lab is down that road to the right," Indigo said, pointing toward the section of campus where she'd spent most of her time during her senior year.

Niko turned down the road and followed it until it came to a parking lot at a dead end. After they parked, Indigo hopped out and waited for Niko before leading the way. Now that she was there, something had come over her, and she felt an irresistible pull toward her former lab. It was as if she needed to see it, smell it, experience it again just to prove to herself that the experience hadn't broken her. That she could go back and not lose herself in the process. It was as if all the rage and disappointment she'd carried with her after being expelled needed to be purged, and the only way to do that was to face the ones who'd failed her.

Memories of Indigo's time on campus came flooding back. All the time she and Tricia had spent walking the grounds, the time they spent in the lab, the parties they'd frequented at the Witchery Society, the club they belonged to that was supposed to help them with connections after they graduated. Indigo hadn't been surprised when all her close girlfriends suddenly disappeared once she'd left school. None of them would want to be associated with a witch who'd gone bad. She couldn't even say that she blamed them. If she'd had limited information to go on, she'd likely have done the same in their shoes.

All the hope and pride she'd felt back then had just disappeared into the ether. She'd hoped she'd be some sort of revolutionary when it came to creating spells and potions. It was everything she'd been focused on since before she'd even started high school.

That girl back then would have been horrified to learn that she'd just moved home and taken over the family business. But now? Indigo was a different person. She loved her close-knit hometown and being near her grandmother and sisters. There was a quiet joy in her work. Bringing enjoyment to the people who visited her shop was more than enough. She'd learned the hard way that ambition wasn't everything.

Niko cleared his throat.

Indigo turned to look at him, having almost forgotten that he was there.

"You seem to be on a mission. Want to fill me in on where we're going?"

She blinked. "I thought you wanted to talk to Polly's adviser."

He nodded. "I do. Professor Cannon. Do you know her?"

"Professor Cannon?" Indigo glanced up at the building in front of them. Then she felt a smile claim her lips. "I thought..." She shook her head. "Never mind. It doesn't matter. I do know Professor Cannon. Come on. This way."

Indigo grabbed his hand and tugged him along with her. In her excitement to see her favorite professor, the majority of her anxiety seemed to melt away. Professor Cannon had been one of only two professors who'd been kind to her after they'd lost Tricia, and Indigo had never forgotten.

When they arrived at Room 312, Indigo paused as she knocked on the open door. The woman sitting at her desk pushed back her long, wavy blond hair and squinted in Indigo's direction. It took her a few seconds, but recognition dawned in her deep blue eyes before she gasped and ran over to Indigo.

Professor Cannon clutched her arm and pulled her inside. Niko was barely in the office when the professor slammed the door shut and turned around, her expression grim as she said, "Indigo, you shouldn't have come."

# CHAPTER 14

"Why is that?" Niko asked, suppressing the urge to stand in front of Indigo as if that would protect her from this professor who clearly wasn't happy to see her. He hated the way that Indigo's entire demeaner had shifted once the professor had opened her mouth. One second she'd seemed eager to speak to Cannon, and the next she looked as if she wanted to vomit.

"Who are you?" the professor asked, frowning at him.

He pulled out his badge and introduced himself. "Agent Niko Morales from the MTF, and I'm here to investigate the circumstances around Polly Smart's compulsion. And Indigo is here because I asked her to be." He cocked an eyebrow, just waiting to see what she'd say.

The professor's eyes widened as she took a step back. She glanced between Indigo and Niko before her gaze settled on Indigo. "They think you have something to do with this."

"Why? This is the first time I've walked on this campus since they ousted me a decade ago." But before the professor could answer, she shook her head. "They are still looking for a scapegoat, right? Anything to sweep the scandal under the rug?"

"I'd guess that's true," Cannon said as she took a seat behind her desk and waved for them to sit. "We've been told to report you if we see you here."

Niko frowned. "Report her to who?"

"The administration." Cannon lifted her hands, palms up. "I'm not sure what they'd do with that information. Pass it on to the investigating officer, I suppose."

"*I'm* the investigating officer," Niko stressed, but he had a good idea of who they might be reporting to.

Cannon pressed her hand to her forehead and let out a sigh. "This is the first I've heard of the Magical Task Force getting involved since everything went down with Polly, but I suppose I shouldn't be surprised. So far, the investigating officer has been with the state."

"It's Paul, isn't it," Indigo said, her voice flat.

Cannon nodded. "He has a score to settle."

"I suppose he does." Indigo looked away, staring out the third floor window.

Niko leaned forward. "Just so you are aware, Officer Pitts doesn't have authority over this case anymore. The MTF has taken it over, and I'm the only one with the authority to bring charges. Understood?"

"Yeah, that makes sense, but I think someone needs to tell Pitts that," she said.

"I already did," Niko said. He ground his teeth together,

annoyed. If Pitts didn't back off, there was going to be another confrontation. And while he was normally as diplomatic as possible when dealing with other law enforcement personnel, this time he'd relish putting Pitts in his place.

"Oh. I see." The professor frowned and then said, "What can I do for you, Agent Morales?"

Niko pulled out a small notebook and a pen. "I'm interested in hearing about your last interactions with Polly before she was found in that burning building."

"I've already been questioned about this," Cannon said, her eyes misting with tears. "I wasn't even here when she went missing."

"I know this is emotional," Niko said, using a sympathetic tone. "No one is accusing you of anything, Professor Cannon. I'm just trying to establish a timeline of events so I can track Polly's movements before she went missing."

"Okay." Cannon sniffed and seemed to steel her spine as she held Niko's gaze. "The morning before Polly went missing, we had a meeting to go over her senior project. She was working on a vision correction spell and needed some guidance on how to best test it. We brainstormed ideas and wrote a research plan. Then she left for lunch, and I left for the airport."

"What time did you two part ways?" Niko asked as he scribbled in his notebook.

"Just after 1:00 p.m. I had to be at the airport by 2:15 to get through security," she said.

"Where did you go, and what time was your flight?"

"My flight left at 4:00 p.m. I flew into Boston and then took a rideshare to Salem. I was there for a potions convention. If you need witnesses, I can provide you with a long list. My sister was with me on the plane, and plenty of people saw me at the conference. I was there for four days total."

Niko had no reason not to believe the professor, though he would double check her alibi just to be sure. But all of that was too easily verifiable for someone to make up. "Do you have access to Polly's class schedule?"

"Sure." She tapped on her computer and printed out the schedule in question. "I can already tell you that she was in her Ethics of Witchcraft class that night. It's a once a week, three-hour lecture. Professor Mills has already confirmed."

"How is Professor Mills?" Indigo asked.

Cannon gave her a small smile. "He's well. Just as jolly as ever."

Indigo nodded. "He always had a way of cheerfully delivering a lecture. I never thought I'd miss debating the ethics of spelling inanimate objects."

Cannon chuckled. "Yeah, he's a funny one."

Niko stared down at his notes. "So, Polly was in class until 10:00 p.m. and then wasn't heard from until she was found in that burning building?"

"Yes," the professor said. "Her roommate said she never came home that night."

Niko jotted down the name of Polly's roommate and then stood. Indigo joined him, but she was standing awkwardly like she couldn't wait to get out of there.

"Thank you, Professor Cannon," Niko said, holding out

his hand to her. "I appreciate your time. I'll call if I have any more questions."

"Of course." The professor turned to Indigo. "It's good to see you. The way everything went down back then... It wasn't right."

Indigo just stared at her.

"They never should have pushed you out like that," she continued, her eyes searching Indigo's face. "I wish... Well, you were always an extraordinary witch. I wish you could have stayed and finished your degree. Who knows what you might have become."

"I'm happy with my life," Indigo said, suddenly becoming animated. "I'm not sure pushing students to explore their magic beyond breaking points is really in the best interest of anyone. In fact, I'm pretty sure that Professor Mills would agree."

Cannon suddenly laughed. "You know what? You're right, he would." The woman rounded her desk, wrapped her arms around Indigo, and said, "I'm glad you have someone who finally appears to be on your side. I never once thought you were responsible for what happened to Tricia."

"Thank you," Indigo said, hugging her back. When she let her go, she added, "But I'm not sure that's entirely true. If it wasn't for me, that spell wouldn't exist, and we wouldn't be investigating another incident. But I'm going to do what I can to help Niko find whoever did this to Polly."

The professor looked almost proud as she stared at Indigo and then waved as they left.

"That was… interesting," Niko said quietly as they made their way down the corridor.

"Professor Cannon doesn't have anything to do with this," Indigo said.

"I agree, but someone in the administration here does. It might be time to talk to the dean."

Indigo eyed him, and after a pause she said, "I think you should do that on your own. I have no interest in seeing that man."

Niko thought it over for a moment and then nodded. "You might be right. I can come back."

She waved him off and said, "I'll wait in your truck. Go do what you have to do."

He didn't feel great about leaving her on campus by herself, but when she insisted, he said, "All right. But text me if anyone bothers you or if you feel like it's too much being here. I'll come right out. Understand?"

"I'll be fine." She gave him a forced smile and added, "I am a witch after all."

"That you are." He walked her to his truck, and once she was safely inside, he touched the magical dagger he wore on his hip and strode off toward the administration offices. He wanted to find out once and for all why everyone on this campus seemed to think that Indigo was involved in compelling anyone when she'd been living a quiet life in Befana Bay for over a decade.

# CHAPTER 15

INDIGO WATCHED Niko walk away from the truck as she slumped down into her seat. The rollercoaster of emotions had taken their toll. She'd gone from dread to excitement to disappointment in all of about five minutes, and it had left her wishing she'd never agreed to accompany Niko to the university at all. He hadn't needed her. Not really. It's not like he couldn't have gotten the same information from Professor Cannon if she hadn't been there to be humiliated.

When was she going to learn? People and their biases never changed. Not really. Maybe individuals grew, but institutions? Not in her experience. They just wanted their troubles swept under the rug so they didn't have to deal with them or be embarrassed by them anymore. So the school was right back to blaming her for something she hadn't done. Her only saving grace was that Niko believed in her.

She wondered how long that would last. If he spent

enough time listening to them, would he eventually see her as a suspect, too?

Indigo shook her head, knowing that she was borrowing trouble. Niko had done nothing to indicate he was the type of man who would take the easy road or be influenced by political pressures. In fact, hadn't he become an agent so that he could right wrongs and make sure that innocents weren't wrongly incarcerated?

If there was ever a time to trust someone, this was it.

But why did it have to be so hard?

She focused on the man who'd been there for her after Paul's verbal attack. And how he'd taken care of her after she'd freed both Polly and the woman outside her shop from the compulsion spells. He'd been nothing but honorable and honest. He deserved her trust. She knew that and prayed to the goddess that she could give it to him.

As she sat staring out the passenger's window of the truck, a familiar tingle of magic lightly brushed her psyche, jerking her out of her internal thought bubble. She scanned the lawn, searching for the source of the magic. It didn't take long for her gaze to lock on the two women riding brooms just above a tree canopy on the far side of the field.

They must've been brooms from Brooms that Vroom, otherwise she wouldn't have been able to feel the faint trace of her magical signature in the air. She found herself stepping out of the truck, watching the two women as they road toward the experimental lab building. One had her long brown hair tied back into a ponytail. The other had black curly hair that sparked a sudden memory. It was the same color and texture of the woman who'd Indigo had saved outside her shop only a few days ago. The one who'd disappeared before anyone could question her.

Indigo's feet seemed to move without her permission, carrying her toward the building as the two women landed. The one with brown hair stumbled slightly but then let out a high-pitched laugh that she'd recognize anywhere.

"Kinsley?" Indigo called as she picked up her pace. Now that Kinsley was back on solid ground, there was no mistaking her. Her sleek brown hair glinted in the sunlight as she locked up the two brooms in a broom rack near the building.

The dark-haired woman turned and glanced back at Indigo. Shock washed over her features as she quickly grabbed Kinsley by the elbow and suddenly steered her into a crowd that was streaming out of the building.

"Kinsley, wait!" Indigo called, running now to catch up to the two women. Everything inside of her screamed that she needed to talk to them. Questions flashed in her mind that she couldn't turn off.

Since when did Kinsley know the woman who Indigo had saved from the compulsion spell? Why was Kinsley ignoring her calls and texts? And last, but not least, why were they intentionally trying to lose Indigo in the crowd?

Indigo pushed her way through the students, straining to find Kinsley and her friend. But once the crowd thinned out, she didn't see anyone familiar, much less her MIA employee and the woman she'd helped. She took a long moment to check and make sure she wasn't missing anything. They weren't anywhere outside. The only place they could've gone was into the building. After hesitating for only a second, Indigo sucked in a breath and strode up the stairs and back into the building.

She spent the next ten minutes walking the halls and peeking into all of the classrooms and labs, but she didn't see even a hint of either of the women. Instead, she endured curious glances and a few glares from professors who seemed to recognize her. But before they could say anything, she moved on quickly, knowing full well that the longer she lingered the greater the chance she'd have to deal with Paul Pitts again. If one of them reported seeing her, she'd have to endure yet another showdown with him.

"Indigo?" a familiar male voice called curiously.

She spun and found herself staring into the face of Professor Mathew Mitchell. He had a wide welcoming smile, and his deep brown eyes were sparkling with warmth.

"My goddess, it is you," he said and then wrapped her in his arms, pulling her in for a tight embrace. As he held on, he lowered his voice and said, "I thought for sure we'd never get the honor of seeing you around these parts again."

A lump got caught in her throat as she blinked back unexpected tears. Professor Mitchell was her and Tricia's adviser and had been the one and only person in authority who'd stood up for her after Tricia's death. He'd fought to keep her at school, but after everything that happened, she hadn't even wanted to stay. It had all been too much. Indigo pulled back and swallowed before she said, "I didn't expect to be back."

"Damn administration." He shook his head. "You were the best student these halls have seen in fifty years. The day they cast you out was the day they lost their integrity. I'd apologize on their behalf, but it appears they've learned nothing in the past decade."

Indigo shook her head. "It doesn't matter. I'm only here to help a friend. I don't care about... all that."

"It'll blow over," he said. "Mark my words. And when it does, I'd love it if you'd consider working with me again."

"Work with you?" Indigo was taken aback. "I'm not coming back to school, and even if I wanted to, they'd never consider letting me back in."

"No, that's not what I meant." He gave her a small smile. "I'd like to have you as an assistant with my work. I've been working on some magical medical research, and you'd be the perfect person to help me with that."

"Magical medical research?" she asked, frowning. "You mean like what Polly Smart was doing?"

His brows furrowed. "Wasn't she working on magical vision correction?"

"That's what I was told."

"That's worthwhile, but no. That's not what I'm doing," he said. "I'm working on spells to heal tissue for use in surgeries and medical trauma. It has the potential to save millions of lives."

"That's impressive," Indigo said, vaguely remembering that when she'd been in school, no witch had figured out how to isolate their spells with any sort of precision for such delicate work. If he'd found a way, that was a major breakthrough.

"What do you say? Will you consider it?" he asked hopefully.

She paused, knowing that his work was important, but she also knew that experimental magic, even used in research, was a bridge too far for her. She just didn't trust herself. "Thank you for the offer, but I really don't think it's in the cards for me."

The disappointment in his expression was unmistakable. "If you change your mind—"

"I won't," she said, not wanting to give him false hope.

"I hear you, but if for some reason that changes, you know where to find me."

"Thanks, Professor Mitchell," she said.

"It's Matthew." He squeezed her shoulders affectionately and then walked down the hall toward his office.

Indigo stared after him, wondering what sort of alternate reality she'd walked into. When she realized she was blocking a classroom, she finally gave up on finding Kinsley and her friend and headed back to the truck.

Once she was outside, she walked by the broom rack and paused, scanning the various brooms. Her magical signature had a strong presence, but not one of the brooms were the style that she sold or rented at her shop. Confused, she held her hand out over the brooms. Two of them started to shimmer with magic. Both were basic brooms that one could buy at just about any commercial magical store. What was different about them was that these brooms were infused with magic that held her signature. But not just *her* signature. The magic was mixed with someone else's, too.

Kinsley's. She'd recognize it anywhere.

The only question was, why was *her* magical signature there on brooms she'd never seen? Had Kinsley stolen it the day she'd shown her how to spell brooms? Or had Indigo's magic gotten away from her again?

Rubbing her forehead to combat the growing headache, Indigo let out a groan of frustration and then went to wait for Niko in his truck. This day couldn't end soon enough.

# CHAPTER 16

"CAN I HELP YOU?" The gray-haired assistant peered over her glasses at Niko, her lips pressed into a thin line.

"Yes, good afternoon. I'm here to see Dean Rollins. I'm—"

"I'm sorry, the dean is in a meeting right now. And he's booked up for the rest of the day. You'd be advised to make an appointment," she said dismissively as she went back to tapping the keys on her computer.

Niko gritted his teeth at the blatant dismissal and then cleared his throat. "As I was trying to say, I'm Agent Morales from the Magical Task Force, and I'm here to speak to the dean."

That got her attention. Her fingers froze as she peered up at him. "Do you have identification?"

He pulled out his badge and his agent ID and waited.

"One moment please," she said with a frown as she hurried into the office just beyond her desk.

Niko glanced around at the ornate office. It was filled with dark wood furniture, portraits of stuffy-looking academics, and a smattering of historical witch relics. There was an ornate candelabra on the fireplace mantle and an ancient-looking crystal ball on a pedestal near the velvet curtains that covered the windows. The rug had a large pentagram pattern, and there were dried herbs in a ceramic vase on the assistant's desk. It was tasteful but more than a little bit predictable.

The door to the dean's office swung open. The assistant looked like she'd just sucked on a lemon when she said, "Dean Rollins will see you now."

He gave her a short nod and then swept past her into the musty office. It was nothing like the outer office that was dignified and tasteful. This office was full of stacked books, candle holders with candles that had been burned to stubs, and crystals everywhere. It had the look of a mad scientist who spent more time doing spells and research than someone who actually ran a college.

The one thing that wasn't there was another person. Nor was there even a computer that he could see. Unless he'd been on a conference call on the phone, Niko didn't see how it was possible the dean had been in a meeting.

"Agent Morales," the dean said, steepling his fingertips together. "I hope you are here with good news."

Niko raised one questioning eyebrow. "What news would that be, Mr. Rollins?"

"It's Dr. Rollins," the man said as he stood to his full height. He had to be at least six five, and he towered over Niko by a good four or five inches.

"My apologies, Doctor. If you're asking if we've apprehended the one responsible for compelling Polly Smart, then I hate to be the bearer of bad news. Unfortunately, I'm still trying to determine who would have had opportunity and motive. And that's what brings me here today."

"We know who's responsible," the dean said with an air of importance. "If you were any good at your job, you'd know that, too."

"Oh? You've known this entire time, have you? Maybe I should take you down to the office and question you for withholding information." Niko was just messing with the pompous man. There wasn't any law on the books that said he could be apprehended for withholding information. But Niko sure wished he had grounds to handcuff him and haul him down to the MTF.

The man gave him a flat look as he took his seat again. No doubt he knew that Niko was bluffing.

"Okay, so why don't you tell me who you think is responsible?" Niko asked, even though he was sure he knew where this was going.

"Indigo Easton of course. She invented that spell. She's the only one with the power to wield it. And if the MTF hadn't messed up the case a decade ago, she'd be in prison today. But she's not, and here we are with students falling prey to her depravity once again. Put her behind bars and all of this will end."

"What makes you think Ms. Easton is involved in Polly Smart's case?" Niko asked, doing his best to keep his unmitigated rage in check.

"I just told you, Mr. Morales," the dean said dryly. "She created that spell. She alone has the power to wield it. Look into her actions over the past couple of weeks, and I'm certain you'll find the evidence you need for a quick conviction."

"Why are you so certain that no one else can do that spell?" Niko asked, curious now. The man seemed so sure of his position.

"The only other person who had the knowledge to wield that spell died. Tricia Brighton would be the only other suspect, but she's no longer with us. It's not rocket science, Mr. Morales. Now, if you'll excuse me, I have more work to do before I leave for the evening." He gestured to the door, making it open with just a wave of his hand.

Niko ignored the door and the not-so-subtle command. "What makes you think that no one else has figured out how to do that spell?"

The dean sucked in an irritated breath and slowly let it out before he answered. "Those types of spells are not only highly advanced, but they are also closely connected to the creator. Anyone else trying to work that particular spell would likely either be a victim of the spell backfiring, or the spell would be significantly weaker. For Polly to be so thoroughly compelled, that convinces me that Indigo Easton has emerged from wherever she has been hiding all these years. And if you don't do something about her, this *will* happen again. Mark my words, Agent Morales. Witches become addicted to that sort of power. They don't stop until they are either locked up or they flame out."

Flaming out was the term for when witches used so

much magic that it incapacitated them. That rarely happened. But when it did, it brought a horrifying amount of destruction not only to the witch but to those around them. Niko pursed his lips as he studied the dean. "So you've decided there's no need to investigate?"

"It's a waste of my time and yours, agent. But do what you have to do. Just don't go looking for trouble where there is none, or I'll be forced to report you to your superior for harassment." The dean stared him down, clearly daring Niko to call his bluff.

Niko just nodded once. He'd gotten what he'd come for. He now knew exactly where the administration stood and why. But instead of making him question Indigo, he was now suspicious of not only the dean, but any and all professors who had worked with Polly or with Indigo when she'd been a student. He strode to the door, and just before he left he said, "Thank you for your time, Dean Rollins. This interview has been most insightful."

The dean grunted and said, "I look forward to Indigo Easton's trial."

Niko stared at the old coot for a long moment before he shook his head slightly and left without another word.

He quickly made his way back to the truck, his gut churning with anxiety. After talking to the dean, he was second guessing his decision to leave Indigo alone on the campus. If almost the entire administration had it out for her, there was no telling what could have happened in the thirty minutes he'd been gone.

But he needn't have worried, because he found Indigo

sitting in the passenger seat of his truck, vigilantly scanning the grounds.

"What are you looking for?" he asked as he climbed back into the driver's side.

"Not what, but who. I saw Kinsley and that woman who was compelled right outside of my shop the other day. They were riding brooms together." She nodded toward the broom rack. "I tried to go talk to them, but they rushed off and I lost them in the crowd."

"The woman who took off after you cured her?" he asked, astonished. "She's a student here?"

Indigo turned to look at him, her expression troubled. "I don't know. Kinsley acted like she didn't know that woman the day I reversed that spell, so now I'm starting to think they are working together on something nefarious that has to do with Polly or Tricia or both. But I have no idea what it could be or why it's coming up now. I've had zero involvement with any of this since the day Tricia died. And other than the fact that I've been... I don't know, sort of dating you, I have zero connection to Polly other than the fact that you've been assigned to her case. So why are these people coming to my town and sniffing around me?"

For the moment, he ignored the fact that she'd admitted that they'd been dating and focused on her question and voiced what he'd been thinking ever since he left the dean's office. "It feels like someone is freaked out that everyone knows about Polly's compulsion, and they're trying to frame you for it."

Indigo blew out a long breath. "But how are Kinsley and that other woman involved? Do you really think Kinsley has the power to do a compulsion spell?" She didn't see it. While the young woman had plenty of magical skills, she hadn't felt Kinsley's familiar magic when she'd neutralized the compulsion spell. It had to have been done by someone else.

"That's something for me to investigate," Niko said as he scanned the campus. His first inclination was to scour the grounds until he found Kinsley, but unless he was prepared to go room by room and drag Indigo with him, that wasn't going to be very practical. It was better to set up a stakeout operation and wait for her to go home or to any of her other regular haunts.

"But not me?" Indigo asked, looking resigned.

"To be honest, Indigo, I think it was a mistake to bring you here today," he said. "The dean has it out for you, and there's no telling who else on the staff is as single-focused as he is in pinning this all on you. We need to find out who compelled Polly and that other woman as soon as possible. If not, there's likely going to be a lot more internal pressure to pin it on you. And if Kinsley or anyone else is trying to frame you or plant evidence, things could go south quickly."

"I didn't want any of this," she said, staring him in the eye. "I did this because you asked me to."

"I know." He hated that he'd put this on her. But he'd thought she might be able to bring some insight. And while that hadn't happened, he had learned that no one on this campus had forgotten anything about Tricia's death and the circumstances surrounding it. "I'm sorry for that, but thank you for being willing to help. I'll take it from here."

She sat back and crossed her arms over her chest. "So now that I'm involved, you're cutting me out?"

"That's not—" He shook his head. "I'm only trying to protect you."

She closed her eyes, looking thoroughly done. Finally she said, "I know. I'm just... I thought this was all behind me and here we are again."

He reached over and squeezed her hand and was mildly surprised when she squeezed his back. "I'll solve this case. I promise you that."

She nodded, and Niko put the truck in gear and drove them off the campus.

When they were almost back to Befana Bay, he said, "Everyone at the school seems to think you're the only one with knowledge of this spell, but it seems to me that your adviser would know the details, too."

"Professor Mitchell?" she asked, sounding a little surprised. "You think he's the one behind all this?"

"No," he said carefully, not wanting to jump to conclusions. "I'm just trying to rule out anybody who'd know how to wield that spell."

"That makes sense." She took a deep breath and seemed to think about her answer for a moment before she said, "It's possible, I guess, but he didn't have access to my final notes. He'd been advising us on what might be the best way to go about the spell, but he didn't have my specifics. That's what I was supposed to turn in at the end of the term. After everything went wrong, I locked everything up in my safe and never showed anyone ever again."

"Do you think he could have worked out how it was done?" Niko asked.

She shrugged. "I suppose you could say that about

anyone, but the thing about creating spells is that they are each unique to the witch who creates them. It's sort of like writing a story. If you give everyone the same prompt, they'll all go about it a different way and end up with something unique. But once it's out in the world, it can be taught and copied. I just think that without the minute details, it would be hard to recreate."

"But not impossible," he reiterated, trying to get a sense of how far into the faculty he needed to investigate.

She pursed her lips. "I suppose not, but from my limited experience, I'd say it's unlikely. The only way would be if Tricia brought the spell to him and then he used it on her." She grimaced. "I can't rule that out, but I will say I'd be surprised. Professor Mitchell was never anything other than a complete professional who always rambled on about ethics and how far we should push our magic. This just seems… more than a bridge too far."

Niko nodded, letting her know he'd heard her. But in his mind, everything she'd just said had only made Professor Mitchell his number-two suspect. The dean was number one with his villain-like reaction. Mitchell was next on the list. What better way to throw off the scent of wrongdoing than acting like the jovial, ethical professor who is liked by everyone? The charismatic person who possessed an evil or greedy streak often spent their entire lives flying under the radar just because they were so well liked. Then there was Kinsley and her broom-riding sidekick. It didn't make sense why they'd run off when Indigo tried to talk to them. He'd have to find Kinsley sooner rather than later to get a read on her, too.

"You're going to investigate him, aren't you?" she asked.

"I'm looking into everyone," he said. "It's the only way to do a thorough job."

"I suppose that's the most I can ask for," she said and then turned to stare out the window as they headed back into Befana Bay.

# CHAPTER 17

N ɪ ᴋ ᴏ  ᴘ ᴜ ʟ ʟ ᴇ ᴅ  his truck into an empty space behind Indigo's building and turned the engine off.

Indigo turned to him and asked, "Are you headed home now?"

"That depends on you. Are you free for dinner?" There was a glint in his eye, and a tiny hint of a smile played on his face.

"I'm free for more than that." She pushed the door open and hopped out, waiting patiently for Niko to join her.

He didn't make her wait long. Once he was by her side, he asked, "Should we cook, get takeout, or go to The Salt Circle?"

"Takeout." She slipped her hand in his and led him up the stairs to her apartment. She was one hundred percent done with trying to deny her feelings for the man. After the last week, it was clear to her that if she didn't allow herself to trust him, then she was the lost cause. Because this man had done nothing but protect her from everyone who was trying to pin this crime on her. If she couldn't trust Niko, she couldn't trust anyone.

"Works for me," he said as he tightened his grip on her hand.

Once they were inside, Indigo paused for a moment. She was torn between tugging Niko into her bedroom and rummaging through the takeout menus. But when Niko's stomach grumbled, she chuckled and went to the drawer in her kitchen. She pulled out a handful of menus and handed them to him. "You choose, and I'll call and order."

"Pizza, Italian, fish and chips, Thai, and sushi. Plus there's always The Salt Circle for takeout. Not bad for such a small town," he said, choosing the pizza menu and handing the rest back.

"When there's a film being shot here, there are usually a few more food trucks around, too. Tacos and Cuban and my favorite, the soup and sandwich truck." Indigo pressed her hand to her heart as she remembered the last time she had food from there. "They have the absolute best gourmet grilled cheese and tomato soup. Seriously, they should package and sell it at the general store. They'd make a killing."

"Too bad nothing is filming around here right now. I'd be down for that for sure." He winked at her and she rolled her eyes, knowing he was teasing.

"Just tell me what pizza you want, and I'll get it ordered."

"The buffalo pizza," he said. "And the garlic knots." He frowned. "Unless you have a problem with garlic."

"Me?" She threw her head back and laughed. "No self-respecting Easton woman would ever shun garlic. I'll order extra."

Niko grinned at her while she placed the order and threw in a margherita pizza for herself.

"It'll be here in about thirty minutes," she said as she opened a bottle of red and poured them each a glass.

"Thank you." Niko took the glass and sat on one end of her couch.

Indigo sat next to him, tucking her feet underneath her as she faced him. After she took a long sip and felt her muscles starting to relax, she said, "I can't stop thinking about what you said about Professor Mitchell."

"What's that?" he asked as he eyed her over his wine glass.

"You wanted to know if I thought it was possible that he'd been the one to compel Tricia and now perhaps Polly." The relaxation she'd felt with the first sip of her wine started to wear off as she thought through what she wanted to say. "I admit that it's hard for me to believe that Professor Mitchell is involved in any of this. I certainly don't *want* to believe it." She just couldn't. Not after the way everything went down.

"I understand. People who have charm and charisma often are overlooked as suspects in any sort of crime. No one wants to believe their favorite teacher or uncle or neighbor would do something so heinous."

Indigo frowned, hating that he had a point. But still, sometimes a person just knew when something was off and when it wasn't. Didn't that count for anything? "Where does gut instinct come in?"

He eyed her curiously. "Are you saying your gut says he's innocent?"

"Yes," she said without hesitation. "I heard you when you said you needed to investigate him to rule people out, and I'm not saying you shouldn't. But something tells me that Mitchell is one of the good guys. Out of everyone, he and Professor Cannon are the only ones who stood by me. They'd believed in me. Hell, Mitchell still believes in me. I didn't tell you this, but he even offered me a job today as his research assistant."

Niko's eyes turned stormy as he said, "You aren't thinking of taking that are you?"

"Oh no. That's out of the question. But why would he offer that to me if he'd stolen my spell and was responsible for Tricia's death? That makes no sense to me." Suddenly a deep sadness washed over her as she relayed one last truth. "Besides, if he turned out to be the one responsible for compelling young women, I'd likely lose all faith in humanity."

Niko put his wine glass down and held his arm out, inviting her to lean into him.

Indigo didn't hesitate. She needed to feel the comfort and warmth from someone she trusted. And there was no one besides her sisters and grandmother who she trusted more than Niko Morales.

She chuckled softly.

"What's so funny?" he whispered as he rested his chin on the top of her head.

"Me," she said into his chest. "Isn't it ironic that after all these years of vowing to stay away from law enforcement that I not only end up in bed with an MTF agent, but I start to fall for him, too?"

Niko froze.

After a beat, Indigo looked up at him. "Niko?"

His gaze landed on her lips. And then before she could say anything else, he wrapped both arms around her, pulled her closer, and claimed her mouth, kissing her in a way that made the rest of the world disappear.

Indigo's grip tightened on him, and there wasn't anything in the world she wanted more than this man. To be held by him. To let him transport her into another world where the only spells were the ones made of human touch and connections.

Love.

That's what this was.

Indigo was in love with him, and she knew there was no going back. She only prayed that he'd take that gift and cherish it, because if Niko Morales broke her trust, she knew she'd never be the same again.

They stayed locked in each other's arms as time seemed to stand still. She didn't want to think about spells or professors or ex-fiancés. She just wanted to stay in her carefully crafted bubble with Niko and let herself love someone again.

Niko ended the kiss but didn't pull away as he spoke. "Are you sure this is what you want?"

She smiled against his lips. "I'm sure."

"Thank the gods," he said and stood, holding out his hand to her.

Just as she got to her feet, the doorbell rang. They looked at each other before they both laughed.

Niko strode to the door, paid the pizza delivery person, and then turned to her and said, "I hope you were serious about garlic not bothering you, because now that this is here, I'm gonna have to devour my portion before I devour you."

Indigo's face heated as a smile claimed her lips. "I look forward to it."

INDIGO WOKE WRAPPED in Niko's arms. The sun was streaming in the window, shining on their bare skin, and she couldn't remember when she'd ever felt so content. It was her day off, she had a sexy man in her bed, and there was nothing pressing she had to do. In that moment, her life was nothing short of perfect.

"Good morning," Niko said, his voice gravelly with sleep.

She turned her head, noting his hooded eyes and the sexy stubble shadowing his jawline. "It's a very good morning," she agreed before pressing a soft kiss to his lips.

"No argument here." He gazed down at her as he gently brushed a lock of hair out of her eyes and tucked it behind one ear. "What do you have planned for today?"

"This." She gently pushed his shoulder so that he was lying on his back and then climbed on top of him so that she was straddling him. "Do you have any objections?"

"None." He wrapped his hand around the back of her neck and rose up to meet her in another passionate kiss.

Everything about their connection was fire. Indigo hadn't ever experienced anything like it before. Being with him just felt... right. It was right in a way she couldn't explain, other than to say that she felt whole when he was near.

Niko let out a barely audible growl as he lifted her up and spun so that he was hovering over the top of her.

She grinned up at him, loving that she was able to make him lose even a smidgen of his control. It was powerful and made her feel both sexy and wanted.

His hands seemed to be everywhere at once, driving her mad. And just when she was ready to beg him to take her, the doorbell rang.

They both groaned as Niko rolled off her and lay staring at the ceiling.

"Do you always have visitors before eight o'clock in the morning?" he asked.

The doorbell rang again in a rapid succession, indicating that the visitor could only be one person.

"No, only when Sage shows up," she said, rolling out of bed and grabbing her robe. "That one gets up before the crack of dawn when she's working at the glass studio in the summer. It's easier to work in the hot shop before the temperatures heat up."

"Tell her to take her bucket of ice water and pour it over her own head," he said as he draped his arm over his eyes.

Indigo chuckled. "Go get in the shower. I'll meet you there in a few minutes."

He lifted his arm, his expression full of interest. "The shower?"

"Yes. Now go. I'll get rid of her posthaste."

He jumped out of bed, kissed her soundly, and then disappeared into the bathroom. A moment later, she heard the spray of the shower.

Indigo was still grinning as she opened the door and found not just Sage, but her other two sisters as well. She tightened her robe around her and said, "Something wrong with your phones?"

"Nope," Sage said as she brushed past Indigo and headed straight for the kitchen. She was already making a cup of coffee when she added, "It's yours that needs to be checked. I left three messages and you never responded."

Indigo frowned, wondering where she'd last left her phone.

"Good morning," Prim said, eyeing Indigo's robe.

"Looks like we might have interrupted something." Lily giggled as she peered at Indigo's neck. "Is that a hickey?"

Indigo slapped her hand over the perceived hickey and said, "No!"

Lily threw her head back and laughed. "Just kidding. There's no hickey. But it does look like there might be a love bite."

"Oh. My. Goddess," Indigo said, looking around at her sisters. All three of them looked so similar with their blond hair and slightly delicate features. Meanwhile, she was the odd woman out with her dark hair and curvier figure. If she didn't look like the spitting image of her grandmother, Indigo would've sworn she was adopted. "Why are you here? Just to humiliate me, or is there something important that I need to know?"

The three of them sobered instantly.

Sage brought two coffee mugs from the kitchen and handed one to Indigo. She had her long hair tied up in a neat bun and was wearing jeans and a long-sleeved cotton shirt, indicating that she had indeed been up working in her glass shop early that morning. "Grandmother sent us. She said there are some negative forces focused on you and that we should do a binding protection spell until this negative energy is cleared out."

"She did?" Indigo was slightly taken aback. Her grandmother didn't usually recommend such measures unless she was really worried. She swallowed hard and glanced away.

"Indy?" Prim moved to stand next to her older sister. "Are you okay?"

"Yeah, I..." She grimaced. "I suppose I was hoping that all of this would blow over, but it doesn't seem like I'm going to be that lucky, am I?"

"It could," Sage said, but she didn't sound confident.

"Thanks, sis. That's reassuring." Indigo took a big gulp of the coffee.

"Is that the shower?" Lily asked as she walked toward the bedroom.

Indigo ran and cut off her sister before she could walk through the door. "It is. I was just getting ready to get in before you people tried to knock my door down."

"Really?" Sage glanced at the coffee table and the two empty wine glasses that had been left there when Niko had carried Indigo into her bedroom.

"Okay. That's enough." Indigo waved them toward the

door. "Everyone out. Let me get showered and dressed, and I'll meet you at the coffee shop in twenty minutes."

"Twenty minutes," Lily said with a snicker. "Right. We won't be seeing you for at least an hour."

"Longer if she's lucky," Sage said with a wink.

Prim rolled her eyes. "Okay, that's enough. Indy doesn't need our commentary."

"Thank you, Prim," Indigo said, grateful for her youngest sister.

"What she needs to do is get in that shower before her man turns into a shriveled prune," Prim said.

"Shriveled is the last thing one needs when they have a naked man in their shower," Lily added.

"TMI!" Sage cried as the three of them filed out of the apartment.

Indigo shook her head and said, "Order me a pumpkin bread and a chai latte. I'll be there as soon as I can."

"We'll order it in about forty-five minutes," Sage said as she bounded down the stairs. When she got to the bottom, she turned and said, "Have fun!"

Indigo slammed the door on her sisters' smirking expressions and then went to find Niko.

# CHAPTER 18

IT TOOK ALL of Niko's willpower to leave Indigo to go meet her sisters. They'd stayed in the shower until the water had run cold and then reluctantly dried off and got ready for the day. Niko had an investigation to tackle while Indigo was expected at the café.

He walked her down the street until they were right in front of the coffee shop. "Are you busy tonight?"

Her lips curved into that sexy little smile he'd fallen in love with back in Florida. "That depends. What are your plans?"

"To meet you back here and cook you dinner. I'll bring the groceries this time."

"Perfect." She pressed up onto her tiptoes and gave him a soft kiss before hurrying into the café.

Niko stuffed his hands into his jeans pockets and went to find his truck.

Twenty minutes later, Niko was back home in his office, pouring over the records he'd pulled on Dean Rollins and every professor that Polly, Tricia, and Indigo had taken classes from while enrolled at the university. He pulled the ones that had overlapped with Polly and either Tricia or Indigo. He wasn't surprised to find that there wasn't much turnover at the college. Once professors had tenure, they rarely made moves to other schools unless there were interpersonal conflicts that festered like an old wound.

Still, the only professors in his investigation pile were Professor Cannon, Professor Mitchell, and another named Professor Fields. She taught a Women in Magic class and only seemed to offer it one semester a year.

As a Magical Task Force agent, he had the resources to run instant background checks on just about anyone. The only people who were off limits were those who were high up in the government. With a few clicks on his computer, he had copies of tax records, property records, marriage and divorce certificates, and a full work history.

It took him less than a minute to dismiss Professor Fields. There wasn't one thing out of the ordinary in her background. She was single, an accomplished author who put out a book a year, and taught the one class a year at the college. She lived in a small cottage overlooking the Hood Canal with her two shih tzus and appeared to raise chickens and sell her eggs at the nearby food co-op. There wasn't anything about her that even hinted at someone who'd compel another person to do anything.

Professor Cannon was a little more interesting. Her records were squeaky clean, and at first glance, he didn't see anything that was noteworthy. But then he spotted a car loan, one that Cannon had cosigned on. That on its own was uninteresting. But when he ran the name of the primary person on the loan, he discovered Mr. Justice Keaton had a record. He'd done time in the MTF prison for two years for armed robbery. The weapon was a magical dagger, but it was never actually used.

Niko made a note to visit Cannon to find out her connection to Keaton.

Professor Mitchell's records were also clean at first glance, but once he started scrutinizing his financials, he noted that the man had taken on significant debt in the form of a personal loan right after Indigo had left school. On its own, that wasn't an issue. People took out loans for all kinds of mundane reasons. But this debt appeared to be reoccurring each year for the same large amount. It didn't make sense. Why the same amount every year on the same day for an entire decade? It looked like he'd have to pay Mitchell a visit, too.

He moved on to Dean Rollins. The man had lived and worked in the same place for more than thirty years. He wasn't married. No children. The only thing that stood out was the Rollins LLC on his tax returns. It was listed as sales, but there weren't any other specifics. The company brought in mid six figures a year.

Niko's suspicions went on high alert. What in the world was the dean selling that was making him that much money each year while he spent all day behind his desk at the university? He googled the business and came up with nothing. Then he googled the address on the paperwork and found an empty field.

He'd bet his badge that the LLC was some sort of money laundering operation. After spending ten minutes on the computer, it was evident he wasn't going to learn anything about the business using that route. It was time to investigate the old-fashioned way.

With files in hand, Niko jumped in his truck and headed back to the university.

He found Professor Cannon in her office, reading through a bunch of exam papers.

"Agent Morales," she said, getting to her feet. She glanced past him, looking worried. "Has something happened?"

"No, nothing new." He gestured to the chairs. "Can we sit? I just want to ask a few questions."

"Um, sure." She sat back down in her seat and leaned forward, her elbows propped on her desk. "Shoot."

He cleared his throat. "I'd like to ask you about Mr. Keaton. It's come to my attention that you cosigned a loan for him. Would you care to tell me what your relationship is with him?"

She jerked back, looking as if she'd just been slapped. "Why are you asking me about Justice?"

"He has a record," Niko said as if that explained everything.

Cannon's face soured, making her look like she'd just sucked on a lemon. "Justice served his time. Since he's been out, he's been nothing but a model citizen."

Niko nodded. "That might be true. I certainly didn't find

anything new in his records. Under normal circumstances, I wouldn't be asking these questions, but as you are well aware, Polly was compelled against her will. It's my job to look at everyone connected to her to find out if anyone had motive and opportunity. If I didn't ask about your connection with Mr. Keaton, I'd be derelict in my duties."

She gritted her teeth and looked like she wanted to spit nails. When she finally spoke, she said, "Justice and I live together. We've been in a relationship for the past twelve years. Eighteen years ago, he was with his brother when his brother decided to rob a liquor store. Because Justice had his magical dagger on him, the charges were upgraded to robbery with a deadly weapon. His lawyer was crap, and even though Justice just stood there like a deer in the headlights while his brother demanded the clerk hand over the cash in the register, he went to jail. End of story. Ever since he's been free, he's lived as a model citizen. Now he's a highly coveted dog trainer. Is there anything else you need to know, *Agent* Morales?"

He had to admire her fire. If someone came knocking on his door asking about his past in connection to a crime, he'd probably get his hackles up, too. "He's a dog trainer? Does he not advertise on the internet?"

Cannon's nostrils flared. "No, Agent Morales. He doesn't advertise because he doesn't need to. He gets his work strictly from word of mouth."

"He must be really good at his job," Niko said.

"He is," she said, finally relaxing into her chair. "I'm telling you he doesn't have anything to do with Polly's compulsion. He doesn't even like magic. Not after everything he went through. He spends his days with dogs, and when he has time off, he hikes or bikes the trails."

Niko nodded. It wasn't unusual for former prisoners to develop a love for the great outdoors. After being confined in a cement and brick prison for any length of time, they learned to cherish fresh air and sunshine. "Do you have a current number for him in case I need to get in touch?"

She reluctantly gave him the number.

"Thank you." Niko mimed tipping his hat and then left, intent on finding Professor Mitchell.

Indigo's favorite professor was just ending a lecture when Nico caught up with him.

"Professor," Niko said as he showed his MTF ID badge. "Can you spare a few minutes?"

Mitchell's expression turned from jovial to concerned. "Has there been another incident?"

"Not that I'm aware of. I'm here investigating who might have compelled Polly Smart. Do you have any idea who might have done that?"

"If I did, I'd have already offered that opinion to the investigating officer," he said, sounding annoyed. "Is there a reason why you think I might know something?"

It was the perfect opening. Niko pulled out the papers that highlighted his debt and put them on the man's desk. "Shortly after Indigo Easton left school, you took on a large sum of debt. And while you spend all year paying it off, it seems you take on that same debt year after year. Why?"

The professor's face completely shut down. "My finances are none of your business."

"They are when I'm investigating a crime," he said,

though Mitchell was right. He wasn't suspected of anything, and there certainly wasn't anything to warrant taking him in for questioning. Niko was just hoping that the man would be honest so that he could rule him out and move on, especially given Indigo's fond feelings for him.

"Dammit," Mitchell muttered as his entire face turned beet red.

"Care to share?" Niko asked.

"I'm being blackmailed," Mitchell blurted.

Well now, that was interesting. Niko took a seat and leaned forward. "Why? And by whom?"

"A while back, I was dating a student. Her brother found out and threatened to turn me in to the dean unless I paid him off. It's against policy for faculty to date a student, and if the dean found out, I'd have been fired. I have never loved a job more, so I decided to just pay him. Only the blackmail didn't stop there. He now demands a yearly payment, and I'm not in a position to say no, even if I did want to risk dealing with the dean."

"Why is that?" Niko was on full alert now. There was more to this than a simple payoff.

"The brother is law enforcement and he made it clear that if I didn't play ball, he'd find a way to frame me for something. He's not the bluffing type." Mitchell wore a defeated expression as he glanced away.

A ball of rage formed in Niko's gut. He knew more than one law enforcement officer who abused their position, and it never failed to make his blood boil. "Who is it?"

Michell didn't answer.

Niko stared at him, and suddenly he remembered when

the payments started. "You were dating Tricia Brighton, weren't you?"

The professor jerked his head up, staring at Niko with wide eyes. "How did you guess that?"

"Her brother is Officer Paul Pitts, and since the payments started right after her death, I put two and two together."

"You don't leave any stone unturned, do you?" Mitchell asked.

"No. I don't. And now I have to ask if you knew how to do the spell that Tricia and Indigo created."

"What?" the professor gasped. "You think *I* compelled Tricia?"

"I don't think anything," Niko shot back. "I'm just seeking facts. And the facts are that you were dating a student who was compelled and then died. Shortly after, you were blackmailed by that student's brother. None of that looks good. You must see that."

Mitchell stood so fast that his chair toppled over. "Of course I see that! Why do you think I keep paying that bastard? It wouldn't take much for the administration to decide to pin her death on me. Do you know what a stain that entire ordeal with Tricia and Indigo is on this institution? And the fact that it remains unsolved as to who is responsible for her death only makes it that much worse. Now there's Polly's case, too. If they had a fall guy, they could put this all behind them. It's why they are so desperate to pin it all on Indigo. She's already left. No one will care what happens to her and they can finally sweep it all under the rug."

"And while they are ready to bury her, you're offering her a job. Why?" Niko's instincts told him that the professor was telling the truth, but he still didn't understand why he was trying to lure Indigo back into his world.

Mitchell ran a hand over his head as he closed his eyes for a moment. When he opened them, he stared right into Niko's eyes and said, "I wanted to give her back something that she lost. She deserves the options that were taken from her."

"And?" Niko knew there was more to it than that.

"And I was hoping she could find a way to get me out from under the thumb of Paul Pitts."

There it was. The key that Niko had been looking for. It looked like Officer Pitts had just gone from pain in the ass to criminal and was now officially on Niko's list of people to investigate. "Stay away from Indigo," he warned Professor Mitchell. "If I find out you're trying to use her again, we're going to have a major problem. Understand?"

The man nodded, his face solemn. "You believe me then? You don't think I'm responsible for Tricia's death?" His voice cracked when he said Tricia's name, and there was real pain etched in the lines of his face.

"Did Indigo know you two were dating?" Niko asked.

He shook his head. "We didn't tell anyone. Once she graduated, we were going to make it official. I'd already asked her to marry me." There was no mistaking the anguish in his tone.

Niko knew that romantic partners could have regrets after harming their significant others, but he didn't think that applied to Mitchell. The man just had an open energy that implied he wasn't capable of lying. To confirm, Niko pulled his dagger out of the sheath and nodded when he saw the blade hadn't shifted to any shade of red, the indicator that someone wasn't telling the truth.

"Whoa!" Mitchell raised his hands in the air. "There's no need for that!"

Niko suppressed a chuckle as he sheathed his dagger. "Don't worry. I'm not going to attack you. Just checking the truth meter." He stood. "Thank you for your time. If you think of anything that is relevant to Polly Smart's case, call me. Not Officer Pitts."

"Understood." Mitchell chewed on his bottom lip. "You're not going to tell anyone about me and Tricia, are you?"

"Just Indigo. I don't care about school politics." The man had been dating a legal adult. And if Niko wasn't mistaken, the professor likely wasn't that much older than Tricia. Five years at best. What did he care if they were dating? He didn't. "But you have to understand that if it becomes relevant in solving Polly's case, I'll have no choice but to put that information in my report."

"I don't know what that would have to do with Polly Smart," Mitchell said.

"I don't either," Niko agreed. "But like it or not, the two cases are intertwined due to the nature of the spell, and I don't know what it's going to look like when this is all said and done. So I just thought I should warn you."

Mitchell nodded and bowed his head. When he looked back up, there was a fierce look in his eyes when he said,

"Find out who killed Tricia. I've been waiting for far too long."

"I'll do my best." Niko walked out of the office feeling as if he had the weight of the world on his shoulders. And the day wasn't even half over. He still needed to see the dean and find Kinsley. Plus, now he planned to have a little chat with Paul Pitts.

# CHAPTER 19

"I CAN'T BELIEVE Niko was in your shower the entire time we were there this morning," Prim said, fanning herself with a napkin. They were still at the coffee shop, taking their time sipping their lattes and nibbling on their pastries.

"What I can't believe is that she was in the living room talking to us when she could have been having slippery shower sex instead," Sage added.

Indigo groaned. "Enough. I don't need you three to analyze my sex life, thank you very much."

"Are you sure?" Lily asked, giving her a cheeky grin. "We could give you some pointers."

Indigo snorted as images from the night before flashed in her mind. "I'm sure. Now, our grandmother sent you three troublemakers to me with a mission. Should we get started?"

"Not yet," Prim said as she stood and picked up her paper coffee cup. "We have something else to do first."

"We do?" the other three asked in unison.

They all started laughing.

"Nothing ever changes," Prim said, her eyes glinting with humor.

"That's the beauty of being an Easton sister," Lily assured her.

"Come on." Prim walked to the door and held it open for them. "We're going to have a bonding experience before we do the protection spell. It'll help it solidify better."

"Should I even ask what that might be?" Indigo asked.

When Prim shook her head and stepped outside, Sage slipped her arm through Indigo's and said, "I guess we'll find out soon enough."

"You will and you'll love it," Prim called over her shoulder.

Indigo didn't doubt that was true. Even if it was an activity she wouldn't have chosen, in the end, she'd no doubt feel closer to her sisters. And that was something she was desperately needing at the moment. She was glad to have Niko in her life, but with everything else going on, her grandmother was right. Indigo needed her sisters. With it appearing that her new employee, Kinsley, was somehow involved in the compulsion spells, she needed all the support she could get from people she trusted.

"We're walking to this outing?" Sage called as they trailed Prim down Main Street.

"Yep." Their youngest sister called back.

It soon became apparent what Prim had planned as they walked down the hill to the edge of Befana Bay and found four paddleboards waiting.

"It's a good thing we're all dressed for this," Indigo said, grateful that she'd worn shorts and a T-shirt.

"Please, when's the last time any of us fell off a paddleboard?" Prim asked with a roll of her eyes.

She had a point. For years they'd participated in early morning coven meetings on paddleboards with the other witches of Befana Bay. They were all expert riders.

They all put on their life vests and launched their paddleboards. Prim was in the lead with the other three following. It was a gorgeous sunny day out on the bay. The water was as still as glass with only the slightest breeze.

Indigo glanced around and was surprised to see that no one else was on the water. To have no one around was highly unusual. A feeling of unease started to take over, and Indigo paddled over to Sage.

"Where is everyone?" she asked her sister.

Sage shook her head, clearly just as in the dark as Indigo was.

"Prim!" Sage called. "What's going on? Did you curse the water to keep everyone away or something?"

Prim just gestured for them to keep following her.

Sage, Indigo, and Lily all shared a confused look, but they trusted their sister and picked up the pace to get a little closer.

Finally, they made it to the very middle of the bay, and Prim let her board come to a stop. It was where the town witches usually met for the early morning coven meetings. She met her sister's gazes and said, "Form a circle."

"You mean a square?" Lily asked.

"Whatever," Prim shot back. "You know what I mean."

Indigo took the northern spot on the water with Sage at the south and Lily and Prim at east and west.

"Are you going to tell us what's going on?" Indigo asked her. "Or is it all a surprise?"

Prim laughed. "I asked the coven witches to grant us an hour this morning and they spread the word. That's why no one is out here."

"Why? We're not doing the binding spell here, are we?" Sage asked, glancing around with confusion.

"No. We need the dirt beneath our feet for that," Prim said.

They all nodded in agreement.

Indigo stood on her board, soaking in the sunshine, and then she saw it. The movement in the water as the magnificent black and white creature appeared along with her new baby. The two orcas rose right in the middle of the sisters.

"Oh wow," Lily said, awed.

"Hello, mama and little one," Sage said, crouching down on her board to get a little closer.

Indigo watched the pair with love in her heart. Baby orcas had a hard time thriving in the Salish Sea due to diminished resources. She knew that Prim had brought them out there to cast the protection spell for Arabella and her baby. With all of the recent drama in Indigo's life, it was exactly what she needed. She met Prim's steady gaze and mouthed, *thank you.*

The youngest of the four Easton sisters gave Indigo a faint smile and then raised her hands in the air.

The other three followed suit, and then Prim nodded to Indigo. "Will you lead us in the protection spell?"

"It would be an honor," Indigo said as she focused on the mother and baby swimming in their circle. "Goddesses of water and love, hear our call. Protect this precious mother and daughter and give them the strength to thrive. From north to south and east to west, the Eastons of Befana Bay cast our energy, intentions, and light over these two beautiful souls. Take this offering as a gift and live a long life, knowing that you are blessed."

Magic tingled all around them in a beautiful display of sparkling light that glinted in the sun.

Arabella turned on her side, floating with her daughter beside her as the magic floated down and covered their powerful bodies.

Time seemed to stand still as Indigo was lost in the beauty of the moment. Nothing else mattered but the protection being cast over the two orcas.

Then Arabella and the baby suddenly dove into the water. She quickly reappeared just outside the circle as she emerged just enough to let out a blow, thanking them for their service.

Then they were gone, and the water was as smooth and motionless as it had been when the sisters arrived.

Prim brushed happy tears off her cheeks and said, "I'll never get tired of seeing them."

All the sisters agreed.

Indigo felt an energy inside of her that hadn't been there before. It was a kernel of hope and wonder at the renewal of life and the reminder that there was always something greater than herself. She smiled warmly at her sisters and said, "Let's go get that spell done. I can think of nothing better than to reform that Easton connection."

Her sisters all fell in line behind her as they made their way back to shore.

Once they had their paddleboards stowed, they walked up the hill and the short distance to their grandmother's house. But instead of going inside, they walked through the garden gate and into the wonderland that was their grandmother's garden. There were honeysuckle vines covering the west-facing fence, dahlias, hydrangeas, sunflowers, zinnias, and a variety of other brightly colored gorgeous flowers that covered the half acre of land that bordered an aged wooden path. They followed the path until they got to a round clearing that looked like a perfect spot for a gazebo, but Bethany Befana kept it open so that the family could conjure their spells there in the magic of the garden.

"In the middle, Indy," Sage said as she took the spot on the northern most point of the garden circle.

Lily and Prim stepped on the circle to form a triangle. Immediately white pillar candles popped into existence, hovering in front of each of the sisters.

"It's good to see that our grandmother keeps the garden ready," Indigo said as she focused on the wick of her candle. It suddenly lit with a flame, and then the other three came to life too, powered by the magic of the center candle.

"I'm sure she checked everything this morning before she left for her meeting," Sage said.

Indigo raised one eyebrow. "She's not here?"

"No." Sage picked up a canvas bag that had appeared at her feet. "She said the spell would be stronger if it were just us four. Sister's blood and all that."

Indigo nodded, knowing that was correct. While Bethany Befana was one powerful witch, her strength couldn't match that of the four Easton sisters combined.

"This spell will give all four of us the power to harness each other's magic if need be. It will also bind us together, making it possible to find one another with just a short incantation." Sage looked at each one of them before putting on her deadly serious face. "Are each of you comfortable with possibly giving up your magical control and your privacy for the time being until we know that Indigo is safe?"

Before Lily and Prim could answer, Indigo spoke up. "You know I'll understand if you're not comfortable with this. It's a huge invasion of energy and privacy. If you're not one hundred percent on board, just say so and we'll stop this right now. No hard feelings. I promise."

"I don't like you three knowing exactly how much time I spend at home or in my shop, but it's a sacrifice I'm willing to make," Sage said, her face flushing a mild shade of pink. She was the one sister who had hermit tendencies. In fact, she'd even found herself at odds with their grandmother not long ago because Bethany said Sage was working too much. She'd magically neutralized Sage's power in order to make her live a little. It hadn't gone well, but in the end, Sage had found August and fallen in love, so it hadn't been a total disaster. And while she did work less now, she was still a hermit. She just did her hermitting with her boyfriend… until he dragged her out somewhere.

"I'm in," Prim said with a solemn nod. "Anything for Indy."

Lily was quiet. Too quiet.

Indigo was certain that she was going to back out of the spell. Disappointment clogged her throat, but Indigo put on a patient smile and said, "I understand, Lily, we—"

"It's cool, Indigo," Lily said, cutting her off. "I was just clearing my own energy to make sure I was fully on board. I am now." She glanced at Sage. "Let's get this party started."

Indigo let out a sigh of relief as she watched the canvas bag fly from Sage's hands to Prim's. The youngest Easton sister upended the bag, pouring out a collection of herbs. They clung together in a clump as if they were magnetically connected and floated right in front of Prim. While Prim wasn't an herb specialist per se, she had studied the practice with their grandmother when she was younger, so she was the best one to wield them during the spell.

The best one besides Indigo, that was. Sage was gifted with fire and Lily had a way with words. Indigo was the one who dabbled the most in spells that used herbs and potions. Or at least she had until she'd walked away from the practice after Tricia died.

Indigo stifled a sigh and watched as a wind picked up around them. One by one, the herb bundles broke off the main clump and settled, each in front of one of her sisters. Finally, the last bundles flew toward Indigo and dropped to her feet.

"We're ready now," Sage said, holding her arms out to

her sides. Lily and Prim did the same. They were too far away to be holding hands, but their magic stretched out, binding them each together and binding Indigo to them from the middle of their triangle.

Magic pulsed in the air. Indigo could feel her sisters' magic fusing with her own, filling her up, fortifying her. She felt almost invincible. Throwing her head back, she stared up at the cloudless blue sky and let the magic seep deep into her soul.

"From one to four and four to one, let our will be done," Indigo's sisters chanted.

Their words seemed to come from a far-off distance as they chanted over and over and over again.

And then suddenly, magic funneled into her at a lightning speed, only to have it funnel right back out. But instead of feeling empty, she was warm and fulfilled as the wind and the chants suddenly stopped.

The air was still, and a bird chirped in the distance.

Indigo turned slowly, looking at each of her sisters' flushed and dewy faces and then laughed. "My goddess, it's been a long time since we've done anything like that. I think you've all gotten more powerful."

"So have you," Sage said as the three of them rushed her and folded her into the middle of a hug. "With that energy, I think we'll be spying on you for at least a few weeks."

"Great," Indigo said with a groan, and they all laughed.

They stayed like that in Bethany Befana's garden for what seemed like forever, until finally Prim stepped back and said, "I need to get back to my shop."

Lily said, "And I have an article to edit."

Indigo and Sage said their goodbyes as the two youngest Eastons left the garden.

Then Sage grabbed Indigo's hand and said, "Lunch?"

"Absolutely. Magicking takes it out of a witch."

They both laughed, and without even discussing it, they headed to The Salt Circle.

Two hours later, happy and feeling better than she had in weeks, Indigo climbed the stairs to her apartment, ready to pamper herself a little before her date with Niko. She was just about to let herself in when she noticed the door to her office was open just a crack.

She sucked in a sharp breath as she inched toward the door, certain that she'd closed and locked it the last time she was in there. Was Paul back? Had he come to spy on her? It seemed the most likely scenario, and the very idea fueled her rage.

She briefly considered calling the cops, but her history with them made her hesitate. If she was going to call law enforcement, there was only one person she trusted. She quickly sent off a text to Niko, telling him she suspected a break-in.

Her phone pinged almost instantly with a reply. *Are you okay?*

Indigo quickly tapped out, *I'm fine. I'm outside the door.*

*Do not go into the office. I'm on my way.*

Indigo stared at his message, knowing that she could call on her enhanced magic at any time. She really wanted to know who'd broken in, but she knew it was best to wait for Niko. At best, the trespasser had already left. At worst, they were lying in wait for her. And while she trusted herself and her abilities, there was no reason to put herself in danger over some accounting records and extra inventory.

*What about your spells?* The voice inside her head asked.

The spells in the safe! If someone got to those, there was no telling how many people could be hurt. As much as she wanted to wait for Niko, she just couldn't. It was too risky. Even though those spells were locked up, there were always ways to break charms and locks. She had to do what she had to do.

Without further hesitation, she burst through the office door and then came to a dead stop when she saw the woman crouched down by her safe. "Kinsley?"

# CHAPTER 20

KINSLEY PATTED the floor as she frantically looked for something and then held her hand up as she cried, "Found it!"

"What are you doing here in my office?" Indigo asked as she strode into the room, fuming. This girl just disappeared and then suddenly showed up in her private office? There was something very wrong.

"Oh, Indigo, I'm so sorry," she gushed, looking contrite and a little bit scared. "I came by to talk to you, and when you weren't in the shop, I came up here to see if you were in the office. When I realized you weren't, I was going to leave a note." She tapped a blank sheet of paper that was sitting in the middle of Indigo's desk. "I was just about to start writing when I dropped my pen. And then it rolled under the lip of the safe, and well, you know the rest."

Indigo eyed the pen she had in her hand and then the

paper before glancing back at the door. "Why didn't you just leave a note with Luke?"

She shrugged. "I was already up here."

"But the door was locked." Indigo wasn't buying the story.

Kinsley frowned. "No, it wasn't. I knocked, and when I did, the door just popped open. Are you upset that I'm in here? I mean, I know you must be angry that I didn't come back to work yesterday, and that's why I'm here. To explain why I just left and why I can't come back."

"Why?" Indigo placed her hands on her hips and glared at the woman.

"I got an emergency call from my sister yesterday and had to get home," she said, already inching toward the door.

"That's a lie. I saw you at the university riding a broom with that woman I saved from that compulsion spell. If you're going to explain anything to me, just be truthful," Indigo said, feeling her jaw ache with tension. "Why didn't you tell me you knew her?"

"You saw me yesterday?" Kinsley asked, her voice going up a few octaves. "Where? At school?"

"Yes, at the school. I already—"

"I have to go!" She ran out of the office before Indigo could even think about stopping her. When her brain kicked in, Indigo went to the door and watched as the woman jumped into her car and sped away.

"Looks like I'm going to need a new employee," Indigo muttered to herself and then closed the door and locked it before she went to her safe. It appeared to be just as she'd left it. No one had tampered with it. And when she used her biometrics to unlock it, all her journals were right where they were supposed to be.

The door suddenly burst open, and Indigo jerked her head up. But instead of finding Niko coming to her aid like she expected, she found Officer Paul Pitts standing in her doorway with his weapon drawn. "On the floor. Now!"

Indigo dropped her journal and raised her hands as she stared at Paul, her mouth open.

"I said get on the floor," he yelled, coming closer as he waved his gun.

"Paul, I—"

"Don't make me shoot you, Indigo," he said through clenched teeth.

She flopped to the floor, face down, hoping she'd be able to talk some sense into him. With her arms outstretched, she turned her head to look at him. "What's going on, Paul?"

"It's Officer Pitts, and you're under arrest for theft in the first degree and breaking and entering." He started to recite her *Miranda* rights while Indigo stared at him in confusion.

"What?" she asked, thoroughly baffled. "I didn't break into anywhere or steal anything. What in the world are you talking about?"

"You'll be questioned at the station," he said as he sat on her legs and proceeded to handcuff her.

Indigo could tell the restraints were not magically binding, and if she wanted to, she could call on her sisters' magic to get herself out of them, but that would only make things worse. Then they'd likely slap her with resisting arrest. Until he was willing to tell her the evidence they thought they had on her, there wasn't much she could do but cooperate. "Can I at least call my lawyer to have him meet me at the station?"

"You'll get your phone call after you're processed," he said and then stood and yanked her to her feet.

"Indigo!" Niko called as he burst into the office.

"I'm here," she muttered with relief as she stumbled over her leatherbound notebook that was on the floor near her feet. The one that held all her secrets.

"What the hell is going on in here?" Niko bellowed. His eyes narrowed on Paul. "I thought I told you to stay away from Indigo. She's helping me with my case. If you keep interfering—"

"I have a warrant, Agent Morales." Paul flashed a piece of paper at him. "This doesn't concern you, and I suggest you get out of the way before I arrest you, too."

Niko snorted, but he clearly wasn't amused. "I'd like to see you try it, Pauly."

Paul let out a growl as he pulled his gun from his holster where he'd stored it after pointing it at Indigo.

"I wouldn't do that if I were you," Niko said calmly. "If you point that thing at an MTF agent, it will trigger an internal investigation, and I'm sure you don't want that pesky secret you're keeping out in the open."

"Secret?" Indigo asked, staring at Paul. "What secret?"

"Shut up," Paul spat and yanked on Indigo's wrists as he tugged her toward the office door. "Ms. Easton is under arrest. If you stand in the way, I'll have you arrested, too."

"Perfect. I'm sure your chief will be interested to hear all about the blackmail you've been engaged in for the past decade. I know cops usually protect their own, but since this involves the Olympic Witches University, I'm pretty sure the MTF will be getting involved."

Paul froze, and his tone was like ice when he asked, "Where did you hear that?"

"Why are you arresting Indigo?" Niko countered.

"Who are you blackmailing, Paul?" Indigo insisted, her heart racing. "Do you know who compelled Tricia?"

"No!" he shouted at Indigo. "You're to blame for her death. No one else."

"Then who are you blackmailing, Paul?" She felt like she was going to come right out of her skin. All this time he'd been making her feel like she was the scum of the earth, and it turned out that *he* was the lowlife.

"Professor Mitchell," Niko said. "He was dating Tricia. Paul found out after her death and started blackmailing him in exchange for not outing him to the administration."

"That's a lie!" Paul snarled at Niko. "You can't prove anything."

"You'd be surprised at what records I have access to at the MTF," Niko said mildly.

Paul let out a growl of frustration. "What exactly am I supposed to do here? I have a warrant for Indigo's arrest. I can't come back empty handed."

"Why don't you tell us what you think she did?" Niko asked mildly, clearly understanding that he'd just gained the upper hand.

"He said theft in the first degree and breaking and entering," Indigo told Niko. "I have no idea what he's talking about."

Paul held the warrant out and Niko took it. He

scanned the paper and then handed it back to Paul. "This is easy. Did anyone even ask Indigo where she was last night?"

"We were going to do that at the station," Paul said with a sniff.

"Well, now you don't have to," Niko said. "I'm her alibi. I was here last night with her during the supposed breaking and entering, which means it's impossible that Indigo stole those computers. I'll sign a sworn statement." He pulled his dagger out of the sheath. "See that? No discoloration. It means I'm not lying."

Paul eyed it, and then with a look of defiance he said, "I'm not blackmailing anyone."

The dagger turned blood red.

Niko gave him a sinister smile. "Care to rephrase?"

The two men glared at each other until finally Paul jerked Indigo's wrists again, only this time he pulled them closer to him so that he could unlock the handcuffs.

Her arms sprung apart and started to tingle as the blood rushed back into her hands. Indigo let out a sigh of relief, rubbing her wrists with her tingling fingers.

Niko reached over and pulled her toward him. He never took his gaze from Paul. "I told you before and I'll say it again. Leave Indigo alone. She's not your suspect. If you don't, then you might find yourself in the middle of a nasty internal affairs investigation. Understood?"

Paul just sniffed and then stalked out of the office.

Niko followed him and watched from the door.

When Indigo finally heard Paul's footsteps fade from the stairs, Niko closed the door and returned to her. He pulled her into his arms, holding her tightly as he smoothed her hair. "Are you all right?"

"I am now. Thank you," she said into his chest. Through the entire ordeal with Paul, she'd maintained her cool, ready to deal with whatever garbage he threw at her, but now that it was just her and Niko, she started to tremble.

"Let's get you next door and get some food in you. That will help with the adrenaline rush," he said.

Food was the last thing on her mind as she fumbled stuffing her journal back into the safe. But once she was done, she let him lead her outside. She paused and placed her hand over the office's broken door lock and was grateful when her magic kicked in, repairing it instantly. And thankfully all it took was touching her doorknob for her apartment door to open because she was fairly sure that her fingers were shaking too much for her to manipulate her keys.

Once they were inside, Niko led Indigo to her couch and then went to get her water and a leftover slice of pizza. She watched him, realizing it was the first time in years that she'd had someone to take care of her when she needed it.

"Here," he said as he sat down next to her.

"Thanks." She took a sip of water and one small bite of the pizza. She had a hard time getting it down, but she had to admit that the carbs did seem to help stabilize her. She ate a little bit more before she put the plate down and turned to Niko. "So... That was exciting."

He let out a huff of humorless laughter as he pulled her into him again.

Indigo clung to him. "Thanks for coming when I texted."

"I will always come when you need me," he said. Then he frowned. "Was Pitts the one who broke into your office?"

"No," she shook her head. "I know you told me not to go in before you got there, but I was thinking about the fact that I have my spells in my safe, and I couldn't afford for anyone to get their hands on them. So I burst in."

"Indigo," he said as he squeezed his eyes shut, looking pained. "Do you know how dangerous that was?"

"Yes," she said soberly. "I do. But just to put your mind at ease, my sisters and I did a connection spell today. If I get into serious trouble over the next few weeks, I'll be able to draw on their power."

He raised his eyebrows. "You can do that?"

She smiled. "Yes, *we* can do that. It takes all four of us. It was my grandmother's idea. With everything going on, she wanted me to be protected."

"That's something at least," he said. "Still, wait for me next time."

Indigo didn't make any promises and instead filled him in on what went down before Paul so rudely tried to arrest her. "It was Kinsley. She said she was trying to find me to tell me why she can't work here anymore and was going to leave me a note."

"She was in your office though. Isn't that unusual?" Niko asked.

"It is. No one uses that office but me," she said. "I also found her crouching in front of my safe. She said she dropped a pen."

"Do you believe her?" he asked as he draped an arm

along the back of her couch and leaned back, getting more comfortable.

"No, and when I told her I saw her on campus yesterday, she tore out of here faster than a scalded cat."

"It sounds like she didn't expect to be spotted," Niko said.

Indigo nodded, though she wasn't sure how to interpret what had happened before Paul showed up. Kinsley had been nervous about something. Maybe even anxious. Though Indigo supposed she might be too if she'd just been caught breaking into someone's office. "We need to find Kinsley and figure out what's going on with her and that other woman I saved from that compulsion spell. I think she might have been trying to get to my spell books, but I don't know why. I don't think she's the one who has been compelling people, but she might want the spell to fight back."

"I think anything's possible at this point," Niko said. "And you're right. I need to interview her as soon as possible."

"You mean *we* need to interview her," Indigo said.

"No, Indigo. You need to stay here where you're safe."

She stood, her body no longer shaking. "Because I was so safe just a half hour ago? Don't you think I'll be safer with you?"

Niko stared up at her, shook his head, and then stood and said, "You're right. You're safer with me. Let's go."

# CHAPTER 21

"I HAVE KINSLEY'S ADDRESS," Indigo said as she scrolled through her phone. "It's on file from when she applied at the shop."

"I don't need it," Niko said as he sped down the highway.

"You don't?" she asked, giving him a curious look. "What, did you memorize it from a background check or something?"

"Not quite," he said with a chuckle. "I haven't had a chance to run a background check just yet. I was going to do it tonight, but things have taken a turn."

Indigo was silent as she raised a questioning eyebrow.

"I gave her a ride home that night we took the broom ride when her sister couldn't make it to pick her up," Niko explained.

"Oh." The word came out flat, full of judgment as Indigo turned to stare out the window.

Niko couldn't help it. He laughed. "You're not jealous, are you?"

"No," she muttered.

"If you say so." He swallowed the chuckle that was bubbling up in his throat. "Listen, I was just trying to be nice. I gave her a ride because it was pouring rain and she was stranded after we went riding over the bay, but it was so awful that we cut the night short, and that was the end of that. I do not and never did have a thing for Kinsley."

She turned to eye him and scowled. "You don't have to look so amused."

He instantly schooled his features but knew the smile was creeping back in. "Sorry."

Indigo huffed out a laugh. "No you aren't. You're really enjoying this."

"It's sort of amusing." He reached over and took her hand in his. "You should know by now that I'm all in on this. You and me."

"I know," she said, her demeanor softening. "I just don't like thinking of you with... her. Or anyone else really."

He winked. "Right back at ya, Indigo Easton."

Ten minutes later, they pulled into the parking lot of Kinsley's apartment building. After checking the unit number, they climbed the stairs to the third floor unit and knocked.

There was no answer.

Niko knocked again, but this time he peered into the window as his knuckles hit the metal door.

"It doesn't look like anyone is home," Indigo said.

"I'd say you're probably right." Niko took in the flyers on

the Welcome mat and the cobweb that had formed over the right corner of the doorframe. "Looks like she hasn't been home for at least a few days."

"A few days? I just saw her yesterday and today. Do you think she's staying at a boyfriend's house or something?" Indigo asked.

"I didn't get the impression that she had a boyfriend," Niko said. "Not when she was hitting on me, anyway."

Indigo scowled but then shook her head as if scolding herself for showing she was bothered.

Niko laughed.

"Shut up." She chuckled softly. But when she sobered, she said, "You're right. After you rejected her, she moved on to Mateo. I doubt she has a boyfriend."

A young woman walked out of the adjoining apartment and glanced over at them. "Are you looking for the Coats sisters?"

"Sisters?" Indigo asked. "They live here together?"

"Yeah," the petite brunette said. "Kinsley and Kimber. Twins. But I haven't seen either of them in over a week."

"A week?" Indigo repeated.

The neighbor nodded and waved as she descended the stairs.

"Now what?" Indigo asked.

"We go in and check it out," Niko said as he pulled out his dagger. "Two college-aged women are missing and haven't been seen by their neighbor in over a week? And one might be connected to a compulsion case? Seems like a wellness check is in order."

"We're breaking in?" Indigo asked, looking surprised.

"Sort of. Just to make sure everything is okay." He gave her the tiniest of winks before he pressed the dagger to the lock. There was a soft click, and then Niko turned the knob and pushed the door open. "Stay out here until we know for sure there's no one home."

He walked in and called, "Hello? Kinsley? Kimber?"

There was no answer, and the apartment was dark in the twilight. He quickly searched the two bedroom rental, and when he was certain they were alone, he waved Indigo in.

"What are we looking for?" Indigo asked.

"Clues on where we might find Kinsley," he said as he scanned the apartment. "If there's any mail lying around, look through that."

"That's a federal crime," she said from her spot near the door.

He smirked. "It's not if you don't open it or steal it. We're just browsing."

"Oh." She moved to the kitchen and said, "Found a pile."

He nodded and continued to study the contents of the apartment. A framed picture on one of the end tables caught his eye. He picked it up to study it. Right in the middle were Kinsley and her twin. They were surrounded by five other people. All of them were wearing matching T-shirts with the same logo and the words *The Purple Cauldron*. There was a shelf of alcohol behind them, and he decided The Purple Cauldron was likely a bar. He snapped a photo of the picture before turning around to find Indigo still going through the mail. "Find anything interesting?"

"Yes," she said, looking up, her eyes haunted. "There's mail here for Polly Smart."

"What?" He crossed the room in two strides and looked at the mail in Indigo's hands. "What did you find?"

"It's just catalogs and advertisements, but she was clearly using this address even if she didn't live here," Indigo said. Then she pointed at a box on the kitchen bar. "And deliveries. Look."

Niko scanned the name on the small cardboard box. Sure enough, it was addressed to Polly Smart. "Look everywhere for anything else related to Polly."

"On it."

The two of them scoured the apartment but came up empty. It wasn't until they were about to leave when Indigo spotted another picture. "Look, Niko."

There was a small, framed photo of just the twins and Polly Smart. They were hugging with their cheeks pressed together, and it looked as if all of them had just been laughing.

"So Polly is a friend who was sending her orders here?" Indigo speculated.

"It's possible she was staying here, I suppose," Niko said. "But it's more likely she's just a friend who spent a lot of time here." He wanted to find the twins now more than ever. His gut was telling him that they had the answers he was looking for.

"Now what?" Indigo asked.

He glanced at the time on his phone. "Are you interested in getting a drink?"

"Like at a bar?"

"Yes. The Purple Cauldron to be exact," he said, showing her the picture of the twins. He knew he shouldn't take

Indigo with him on his impromptu stakeout, but he wanted to see if either twin still worked at the bar, and he didn't want to wait another night to find out.

Indigo grinned. "Let's go."

The parking lot was nearly full when Niko pulled his truck into the gravel lot. They parked and followed a young crowd of twenty-somethings into the local college bar.

Niko wrapped an arm around her shoulders and tugged her into his side. "Look like you're here for a good time," he whispered.

"I *am* here for a good time," she whispered back.

Gods, he loved spending time with her, even if he was investigating a case. Indigo was just fun.

They got a couple of curious glances as they navigated their way through the crowd to get to the bar, but most of the patrons were too invested in their drinks and their dates to care about two thirty-somethings who looked like they were dressed for a night in while streaming a movie instead of checking out a trendy bar with the younger crowd.

There was only one open seat at the bar, and Niko led Indigo toward it. He sat and patted for her to sit on his knee. Then with his arm wrapped around her waist, he signaled to the bartender. The bartender nodded that he saw them as he mixed a bunch of drinks for the customer in front of him.

"Kinsley isn't here," Indigo said.

"Neither is her sister, but we'll ask the bartender when he saw them last."

It wasn't long before the tall, dark-haired man who was

covered in tattoos appeared in front of them. "What can I get you tonight?"

Indigo inquired about which beers were on tap and went with the local amber.

"I'll have the same," Niko said.

"Coming right up."

A few moments later, Niko was pulling out his cash as the bartender placed their beers in front of them. But before he handed it over, he asked, "Do you know Kinsley and Kimber Coats?"

"The twins? Sure. Everyone around here does," he said with a grin. "Why?"

"Kinsley Coats is a friend. We haven't been able to get ahold of her or her sister. So we're just trying to connect with either of them while we're in town," Niko said smoothly, making his tone nonchalant. "Do you know where to find them?"

The smile fell from the bartender's lips as he considered the question. "Kimber quit a few weeks ago. But Kinsley? She's supposed to work tomorrow. That's probably your best bet to catch her. Her shift starts at five o'clock, which should be just about perfect for you. The seniors appreciate the happy hour here."

Niko snorted an amused laugh, while Indigo glared at the bartender as he walked away.

"Did he just call us seniors?" Indigo asked.

"It seems like it." Niko held his beer up to hers. "To going to bed at nine and getting discounts at the movie theater."

She giggled.

For the next thirty minutes, they sipped their beers and took in the scene at the bar. Niko didn't see anything particularly interesting. It was just like every other college bar he'd ever seen, except for the large cauldron that was in the middle of the place and advertised a special witches brew. From what he could tell, the brew was just a large vat of mai tais that had been treated with dry ice, but the college students seemed to enjoy the novelty of it.

Once he was done with his beer, he said, "Ready to go?"

Indigo nodded and stood. She placed her empty glass on the bar and held Niko's hand as he led her outside.

Just as they were getting into his truck, he spotted an older man with white, wiry hair poking out from under a fedora walk up to the back door. Niko felt a tingle of recognition wash over him, and he just knew the man was someone he should recognize. He hadn't seen his face, but the energy, no matter how faint, was familiar. The man pressed his hand right in the middle, causing the door to automatically swing open. A second later, the man walked in and the door closed swiftly behind him.

"Was that the dean?" Niko asked.

"Dean Rollins?" Indigo threw her head back and laughed. "At The Purple Cauldron? I think you need to get your eyes checked. Have you met the man? He'd no sooner go to a college bar than dance naked in the quad."

Niko nodded. "You're probably right. He just had an air about him that made me think he looked like the dean."

"You mean musty self-righteousness?"

"That's one way of putting it," Niko told her, completely amused.

"It's the only way of putting it. Now, are we done investigating tonight? I'm pretty sure I was promised a homecooked meal."

"You definitely were," Niko assured her. And then he put his truck in gear and took Indigo home. The sleuthing would have to wait until morning. He had dinner to cook.

# CHAPTER 22

It was early when Niko left Indigo's house the next morning. He'd woken just before sunrise and kissed her goodbye, promising to pick her up after work before he went back to The Purple Cauldron to interview Kingsley. In the meantime, she had to open the store and he was going to continue to research his list of people of interest.

He knew he didn't really have much of a handle on the case. There were far too many questions and hardly any answers. That was likely why the MTF had handed him the case to begin with. He'd made a reputation for himself while dealing with cold cases. The latest was taking down Braxton's ex for years of crimes.

A light rain fell as Niko drove along the two-lane highway back to his house. He hadn't spent much time there over the last few days, preferring to stay with Indigo, but he had to get back to his computer and files. Something told him if he looked hard enough, he'd find a connection he'd been missing.

He came to a stop at a traffic light and suddenly felt a sense of dread. An image of Indigo sleeping flashed in his mind. She was curled up in her bed, a small, contented smile on her lips. That sweet expression was exactly the one she'd worn that morning before he'd woken her to kiss her goodbye. But then the vision shifted, and Indigo was sitting straight up in bed, her hand pressed to her barely covered chest as she screamed bloody murder.

Niko grabbed his phone and hit her number. His truck filled with the sound of the phone ringing. The noise echoed around him, making his stomach churn with bile.

*Ring. Ring. Ring.*

He was just about to run the red light and head back to her apartment when she finally answered in a breathless tone.

"Hello? Niko?" she said, huffing and puffing as if she'd run a marathon.

"Indigo. Are you all right?" he asked as the light turned green.

"Of course. Why wouldn't I be?"

"I just... I had a vision, and it wasn't a good one." He swallowed the lump in his throat. "What are you doing right now?"

"I just got out of the shower. I thought I'd go get coffee and pastries for me and Luke before I opened the store." Her tone was cautious now. "What kind of vision? Do you get those a lot? How worried should I be?"

The fear that had seized his body eased, but he was still chilled all over. He turned his heater on and decided that he just might be losing his mind. "It was a vision of you waking from a peaceful sleep and suddenly screaming. I didn't see anything else. And no. I never get visions. That's why it freaked me out. It felt... very real."

Indigo was silent for a long moment. "I believe in paying attention to visions. It's possible that happens in the future."

"I suppose," he said as he turned into the driveway of his little blue house. "But it doesn't make me feel better about leaving you today."

"What are you going to do? Come back and hang around my shop all day?" she asked, her voice lighter with just a hint of amusement. "I'm pretty sure that won't do much to help you solve your case."

"No, but I'd feel better." He killed the engine and hopped out of the truck, seriously contemplating grabbing his computer and heading back to Befana Bay.

"Me too, honestly, but I'll be okay." Her tone was sober now. "I've got the power of the Easton witches behind me. Go do your thing and get justice for Polly. I'll be here tonight, ready to go with you to talk to Kinsley."

"Yeah, okay. Just be careful, all right?" he said, knowing that she wasn't a helpless wallflower. The entire reason that Indigo was being blamed for Polly's compulsion was because she was a powerful witch. She could take care of herself. But he didn't have to like it.

"I will. You be careful, too, Niko. Just because you're a badass MTF agent doesn't mean I don't worry about you."

He smiled at that. "You think I'm badass?"

"Don't get a big head," she said, and he could practically hear her roll her eyes. "Get to work. Call me if you find out anything."

"Yes, ma'am." He found himself smiling when he ended the call, but as much as he wanted to shake that feeling of unease when it came to Indigo's safety, it was still there, lurking in the back of his mind.

He walked into his stale-smelling house and immediately opened the blinds and windows to let light and fresh air in. Then he went to find coffee before he settled in at his desk to go over his notes.

He stared at his list of people of interest. He'd mentally crossed out Professors Cannon and Mitchell. Neither had given him any reason to think they were involved in spelling Polly. Cannon's only questionable action was dating an ex-con who'd been caught up in a crime against his will. That was hardly a reason to believe she was spelling students. And Mitchell, while misguided, hadn't actually done anything illegal. Unethical? Sure. But people fell in love under inconvenient circumstances all the time. That didn't make them criminals.

That left Dean Rollins, Paul Pitts, and Kinsley Coats on his radar. When it came to Paul Pitts, it appeared to Niko that all he wanted was revenge against Indigo. Would he have waited ten years to frame her for compelling students when she wasn't even part of that world anymore? That seemed unlikely. Niko was convinced he was just seizing the moment after years of growing resentment.

As for Dean Rollins, Niko still needed to look into his

suspicious LLC. He'd planned to go by the address that was listed on the business records the day before, but he'd gotten the call from Indigo and had abandoned that plan. Once he knew what that business entailed, he'd have a better idea if the dean was someone he needed to investigate further.

He typed Kinsley Coats into his list and let out a sigh. He just didn't know what to make of Kinsley and her sister. Or the fact that they seemed to be good friends with Polly. Was it possible they'd figured out how to wield the compulsion spell and things had just gotten out of control, and now they were trying to cover their tracks? Is that why Kinsley had showed up at Indigo's shop, to try to get information out of her? But as far as Niko knew, she'd never asked questions about Indigo's ability to compel people. Though she had been there the day Indigo saved that woman outside the shop, and apparently Kinsley knew the woman since Indigo had spotted them together on campus.

He just didn't have any answers when it came to Kinsley Coats. All he knew was that he needed to look deeper. He spent the next hour running background checks on Kinsley and Kimber Coats as well as Polly Smart. The results weren't very informative. All he got back were hits on spotty work history and average credit reports. That wasn't surprising. They were young college students who didn't have long paper trails. He'd have to call Polly and see if he could get answers. Then he'd stick to his original plan of hopefully catching Kinsley at the bar that night.

After downing the rest of his coffee, Niko picked up his phone and called the number he had on file for Polly.

Predictably, it went straight to voicemail. No one ever answered their phones anymore. He left a message asking if she could call back at her earliest convenience and then sent a text as well. A quick search got him her parents' number. He'd call them next if he didn't hear back from Polly that day.

With his leads mostly exhausted, he grabbed his keys and went back out to his truck. It was time to find out what was going on with the dean's LLC.

Twenty minutes later, he drove by the empty lot that was listed as the address of record for the LLC. It was nothing but a grassy field with a gravel parking lot at one end and one small plastic storage shed. He parked on the street and got out to investigate. There didn't appear to be any tire tracks or evidence that anyone had been there recently. In fact, the uneven gravel driveway was ripe with weeds and overgrown vegetation. If anyone had been there recently, it would be evident.

He glanced around, looking to see if there were any eyes or cameras around. There was nothing as far as he could see. There were a couple of cars parked at a warehouse a block down, but no one seemed to be watching anything.

Niko hurried over to the shed, and when he found it locked, he used his dagger to gain entry. It was instantly clear that the trip had been a futile one. The only things in the shed were a push mower, weed killer, and rat poison. He quickly closed and locked the shed and headed back to the campus. It was clear that if he wanted answers, the university was the only place he'd find them.

After he parked in the administration parking lot, Niko

strode with purpose back to the dean's office. But when he got there, the stuffy administrative assistant informed him that the dean had just left for lunch.

"Do you mind if I just check to make sure he's not eating in his office?" Niko asked as he pulled out his badge. Sometimes it was enough to convince people to go along with his suggestions.

The woman behind the desk didn't take the bait. "No, Agent Morales. That would be highly inappropriate. If you want to talk to the dean, you can make an appointment."

He should have been expecting that response. "Fine. When's his next available appointment?"

She tapped a few keys on her computer. "Next Friday at four. But you'll need to be prompt. He leaves every Friday at 4:15 no matter what."

"You want me to wait a week to talk to the dean about a high-profile case?" he asked, his eyebrows raised.

She shrugged. "I can put you on a waiting list and call if he has an opening."

"That won't be necessary," Niko said and headed for the door.

"Do you want this appointment for Friday?" she called. "It will get filled quickly."

"No." He slammed the door on his way out and headed back to his truck, ready for a stakeout.

The first thing he did was verify that the dean's vehicle was in the parking lot. Then he moved his truck to another location that would give him an unobstructed view. Niko would wait there all day if he had to. If there was one thing he was known for at the agency, it was his patience. One way or another, he'd talk to the dean, even if it meant camping out in that parking lot for twenty-four hours.

It was good that Niko kept his truck stocked with snacks and water, because he'd been in that truck for over five hours before the dean made his appearance. He was just about to jump out of the truck to intercept when the dean pulled out a hat and stuffed it on his head.

It was the same hat he'd seen on the man who'd walked into the bar the night before. A tingling sensation shot down Niko's spine, and he knew then that he needed to follow the dean and see where he was going. He held back, waited for the dean to pull out of his spot, and then followed from a safe distance.

The dean made a quick stop at the bank and then retraced his route as if he was headed back to campus. But just before he entered the large gates, he took a right and drove past The Purple Cauldron.

Niko was careful to keep his distance but didn't miss when the dean parked at a house a few doors down from the bar and then backtracked on foot. He once again went to the back of the building, placed his hand in the middle of the back door, and then entered.

There was no doubt in Niko's mind that the dean was running his LLC operation out of the back room of the bar. He just didn't have any idea what that business might be. There was only one way to find out.

Niko put on a black hoodie, made sure he had his dagger, and then walked around to the back of the building. Only when he got there, he couldn't find the back door. He circled the building twice, each time coming up empty.

"What in the world?" he muttered and then felt it. The faint trace of magic. Someone had obscured the back entrance so that he couldn't find it. But why had he been able to see it from his truck? He quickly went back to his vehicle and squinted. If he tried hard enough, he thought he could see the outline of the door, but he couldn't be sure.

Then a large man with multiple tattoos and a black ball cap appeared. He placed his hand on the wall, making the back door reappear. It didn't automatically open like it had for the dean, but a young woman with blond hair answered it, and a moment later, a dolly of plain brown boxes was passed off to the man. The door shut, and the outline faded again.

That explained it. The outline was only visible when someone was using the door.

With his questions answered, it was time to find out exactly what the dean was selling. Niko reached under his seat, grabbed his stun gun and a magical amulet, and went to work.

Once he reached the back of the building, he held up the amulet. Immediately the outline of the door appeared. Niko didn't hesitate. He pulled out his dagger and stabbed the door right in the middle. The entire door disintegrated, leaving him standing in the opening as he stared in at a man who was fuming with rage.

"I told you to mind your own business, Agent Morales," the dean sneered.

Niko pointed his dagger at the dean, intending to constrain him with magical ropes, but before he could mutter the command, he was hit in the back with two lightning bolts of magic. As he fell to his knees, he managed to look back and saw the twins staring at him blankly, their arms limp at their sides.

His last thought before he passed out was *they've been compelled*.

# CHAPTER 23

INDIGO HAD a feeling of unease she hadn't been able to shake ever since Niko's phone call that morning. And when he didn't answer her texts or show up at her apartment after work, she really started to worry.

She knew he'd been planning on going home to do research before he went out to investigate more, but she didn't know where he was headed after that. If she wanted to find him, should she start at his house? See if he'd left clues as to where he'd have gone?

Or maybe she should just go back to the bar by herself to see if she could talk to Kinsley.

Indecision was making her crazy. The one thing she knew she couldn't do was stay in her apartment and wait for news. After grabbing her keys, she hurried out of her apartment and jumped into her red Ford Escape.

She'd just turned onto the two-lane highway that would

lead her toward The Purple Cauldron when she heard a familiar voice right behind her in the back seat.

"Your boyfriend isn't going to get you out of this one, Indigo."

Indigo immediately slammed on the breaks as she steered to the side of the road. "Paul! What the hell are you doing in my car?" she cried before putting the vehicle in Park and turning around to see not just Paul, but the woman she'd helped in front of her shop earlier in the week. "You. What are you doing here?" She glanced from the woman to Paul and back to the woman.

"Indigo, meet Jesse, my fiancée," Paul said, his eyes black with dark magic.

Jesse chuckled. "You look like someone just peed in your latte. You like yours with real caramel, don't you? And a pumpkin loaf on the side. So predictable."

Indigo blinked at her, wondering why this woman knew her coffee order. Not that it mattered. There were more pressing questions. "What is going on? Why are you both in my vehicle?"

"Just drive, Indigo," Paul ordered. "You'll find out soon enough."

"Yeah, when she's being arrested for the murder of her boyfriend," Jesse said with a snicker. "That should be fun. I've been waiting years for his downfall."

"Who are you?" Indigo asked her, trying to keep up with the sinister pair in the back of her car.

"It's Jesse," she said, curling her lip. "Didn't you hear Paul the first time? Of course you did. You want to know why I have it out for Agent Morales. Well, let's just say that he and

I have a score to settle. Of course I had no idea he was on this case when I agreed to help Paul, but it's a nice bonus for me."

"Help Paul do what?" Indigo asked, though it was a stupid question. He wanted her to pay for what happened to Tricia. It appeared he was doing whatever he could to make that happen. She just didn't know the details.

"Enough talk. Drive, Indigo," Paul ordered as he pressed what felt like a cold steel blade to the side of her neck.

"Where?" she asked as she pulled back onto the two-lane highway.

"The Purple Cauldron. Your boyfriend is waiting for you," he said.

"He's having his final drink," Jesse added.

Indigo chose to ignore her taunts about Niko. There was no way they could compel her to hurt him. They could try, but they'd lose. Instead, she focused on Jesse, realizing that the woman was a talker. If she wanted answers, they'd come from her. "Who compelled you that day, and why were you in front of my shop?"

"You haven't figured that out yet, huh?" Jesse asked. Then she laughed. "And everyone told me you were smart. I guess you're not as special as they all think you are."

Who was everyone? Her old professors? Paul? The police? She had no idea what Jesse was going on about. But it didn't matter. She just needed details. "I guess not," she agreed. "Were you just trying to see if I could still reverse the spell or what?"

"Actually I wanted your magical signature. Letting you cure me gave me that," she said with a cat-that-ate-the-canary grin. "Now everyone I've compelled can be traced to you. Isn't that clever? After they found Polly, we knew we needed a new plan of action, so we decided to kill two birds with one stone. We'd cover our tracks, and Paul would get the revenge he's been waiting all these years for."

Indigo thought she was going to vomit. It was true that when two witches shared magic, if one was gifted in harnessing other's magic, they could hold onto that witch's signature for a short amount of time. It was so short most didn't worry about it. But some were able to carry it for longer. Years even. Jesse could be one of those witches.

*Kinsley carried your magic, too*, the voice in the back of her head said. Indigo remembered the brooms she'd walked by at the college. She'd felt a touch of her magical signature, and she wondered if one of them had devised a way to harness power for longer.

Whatever was happening, it was bigger than she could deal with on her own. She tried to quiet her mind as she focused on one thing—her sisters. She pictured them all together in her grandmother's garden. When she had a pure vision of them in her mind, she mentally called out to them. *I need you.*

Her skin tingled with magic, indicating that she'd at least made the connection. But then it quickly disappeared when the blade Paul was holding dug deeper into her skin.

"Whatever you're doing, stop right now or I swear I'll slit your throat," he threatened.

"And what exactly would you tell your superiors? That a woman driving a car backtalked you so you killed her?" she asked sarcastically.

222

Jesse chuckled.

"Shut up. Both of you," Paul snapped. "I'll tell them you were trying to compel Jesse and I stopped you. Your magic is all over her and the others at the bar. No one will question a thing."

That sobered Indigo. "Others?"

"She's really naive, isn't she?" Jesse asked Paul. "I'm shocked you were ever into her."

"She's a really powerful witch, J. You know how that turns me on," Paul said defensively.

Indigo's stomach rolled again. Did she have to be present for this conversation?

"That explains why you dumped her after she quit practicing," Jesse said.

"I dumped her because she got my sister killed," Paul shot back. "If she hadn't messed up the notes and forgot to add a step, I'd have been able to control Tricia after I compelled her. and she'd never have died in that convenience store."

A bone-chilling shiver washed over Indigo as pure hatred took over every ounce of her being. "You're the one who compelled Tricia?" she asked through clenched teeth.

"I can't believe you never figured that out," Paul said. "Who else had access to your spells? I always thought you were smart, but after that, I knew you were just another dumb idiot who didn't deserve me. You knew I needed money to pay off the school debt that Tricia and I racked up. How else was I going to get it? What better way than to compel Tricia to just take it when the owners of the store she worked at weren't watching? How was I supposed to know that she'd go after other stores, too? And when I ordered her to stop, she wouldn't. She was so singly focused the initial command killed her. And that's all your fault because of your sloppy notes."

Indigo couldn't believe her own ears. She'd been engaged to a complete stranger. Paul was evil to the core. Her notes weren't complete because she'd stopped working on that spell. No one was supposed to cast it ever again. Not that she was going to defend herself to the monster holding a knife to her throat. Instead she said, "It sounds like you've perfected the spell if you two managed to compel Jesse and others at the bar."

"No thanks to you," Paul said.

"I'm not compelled anymore," Jesse said. "Thank you for that, by the way. I'm not too proud to say that I was worried for a minute that I'd be controlled by Paul for the rest of my life. Not that I don't like to be bossed around a little, but that's only in the bedroom."

Indigo wanted to stab herself in the ears. But more than that, she wanted to get to the bar so she could help whoever they'd terrorized and find Niko.

"What about Kinsley?" Indigo asked. "Was she part of this?"

"No. We just used her for information before we compelled her," Jesse said, sounding proud.

"Was she compelled the entire time?" Indigo didn't think so, but she had to ask. It was possible that Paul had refined her curse to make it less wooden after they'd cursed Polly.

"No," Jesse said. "Paul and I nudged her to go work for you so that we could get information on you. It turns out that was a wasted effort. All she learned to do was spell a broom. Hardly impressive."

"Pretty sad existence, Indigo," Paul said.

Indigo didn't answer. She liked her life, and as soon as she was done burying these two under the Magical Task Force jail, she'd happily go right back to it.

Just before they got to the bar, Indigo asked a burning question that they hadn't already volunteered the answer for. "Why are you compelling innocent women? What is it you want from them?"

Neither of her assailants said anything at first.

Finally, as she parked her vehicle, Paul said, "Get out. You're about to find out."

# CHAPTER 24

WHEN NIKO CAME TO, he found himself shackled to a wooden beam. His back was on fire from where he'd been knocked out by the power of two witches, but the thing that was most apparent to him was that he'd been relieved of all his magical gadgets. There was no amulet, no dagger, and no stun gun that had been spelled to work even when there was no charge.

The room smelled like stale beer and unwashed bodies, making his nose twitch. It took a moment for his eyes to focus, but when they did, he noted he wasn't alone. There was a round table in the middle of the room with two women mindlessly crushing herbs and heating potions. Neither of them had any life in them, just a single-minded determination to make potion after potion after potion.

He focused on the faces of each of the women and wasn't all that surprised to see that they were the twins, Kinsley and Kimber. Both of them working silently on what could only be illegal potions. No one who was selling legitimate healing potions would be making them in the back room of a college bar. No, this was a drug running operation. If he had to guess, Dean Rollins had decided that it was cheaper and more efficient to compel his workers to make his product than it was to actually pay them and keep them in line.

Other than the obvious problem of the women going missing, Niko understood why a drug runner would want to compel his workers. More control, less costs. It was a win for a drug boss as long as no one missed the girls.

In this case, Niko had been looking for the twins. The drug boss had attracted exactly the wrong person if they were trying to stay under the radar. It was a huge mistake on their part, and once he got out of this, the dean would be having a nice long vacation in a cement cell.

"It looks like your time here is coming to a close," Rollins said as he walked up to Niko. "Your girlfriend just arrived."

Niko just stared at him. The old bastard didn't deserve a reaction.

Rollins chuckled. "I like your fire, Agent Morales. It's too bad our relationship will end today, but rest assured you'll be remembered as someone who went out honorably."

"How's that?" Niko asked, his voice rough from lack of use.

"Once your girlfriend gets here, her magic will take you and the twins out, and then we'll take her out. After that, it will be clear she's been the one compelling students and running this drug operation. She'll be blamed for all of it. I'll be rid of both of you and this scandal that's been dogging my school for years. Then I can regroup and get back to business as usual."

The back door swung open, and in walked Officer Paul Pitts and Indigo. He had her hands tied and a knife to her throat. Behind them there was a familiar woman with curly black hair that he thought looked a lot like the person Indigo had saved outside of her shop earlier in the week.

"As an added bonus," the dean said, "my partner here will finally have the pleasure of ridding the world of his ex-fiancée. I know it's been a goal of his for a very long time. And I like to reward my most loyal."

Niko tested the bindings around his wrists that were holding him to the wooden beam. They didn't budge.

Rollins laughed, the sound sinister. "You don't really think you stand a chance of getting out of this, do you? I'm a very powerful witch, Mr. Morales. It would take something really special to take me down at this stage of the game."

Niko met Indigo's eyes and tried to express everything he was feeling in that one look. Regret. Determination. Trust. Devotion. He wasn't ready to give up, and he could tell by the look of pure defiance in her gaze that she wasn't either. They'd fight this to the end and die trying if they had to. Not only for themselves, but for the twins as well. He didn't know their role in any of this, but whatever it was, it didn't deserve death as part of a coverup for a corrupt old fool who didn't value anything in life over money and power.

"I'm ready, Dean Rollins," the woman behind Paul said.

"I'm sure you are, Jesse," the dean said affectionately as

he walked over to Paul and the woman. "But first we need to hear from Ms. Easton."

Indigo glared at him.

"Tell us why you think Mr. Morales deserves to die," he taunted.

"I think you deserve a swift kick in the nuts," she said.

The woman he called Jesse let out a bark of laughter. "She really is fire, isn't she, Paul? I can see why you thought she might be your match at one time."

"That's enough, Jesse," the dean snapped as he pressed his hand to Indigo's throat. "As for you, I won't tolerate any more of your smart mouth. Keep it up and you'll find out what it means to be mute before Paul ends your sad existence."

Hatred poured off Indigo, and for a moment, Niko thought she might spit in his face. But instead she just cut her gaze to the twins. There was compassion there, and Niko knew then that there was no way the dean would ever break her. He felt a swell of pride and again tested his restraints.

The dean spun around and glared at Niko. "Stop testing me."

That was when Niko realized he wasn't being held with traditional restraints. He was being held by the dean's magic. If he wanted to get out of this, he'd need to rattle the dean so that he could weaken the spell just enough to break his bonds.

"Am I interrupting your ego-wanking, Dean?" Niko taunted. "It isn't enough to kill us all, you need to make yourself feel all powerful first by insulting a bunch of women?"

He pulled his hand from Indigo's neck and held it up, miming choking Niko. The pressure was instant, though not so tight that he couldn't breathe. "Are you going to kill me, Dean?" Niko choked out. "Go ahead. I'm betting that you aren't carrying Indigo's magical signature. The MTF would go crazy investigating you if they find you killed one of their agents with your bare hands."

Rollins dropped his hand instantly and turned to Paul. "Get this over with."

Paul nodded once and gestured to Jesse. "You're up, babe. Make it good. We're all ready for the show."

Jesse pulled out a couple of small vials of potion as she walked over to the twins. She sat across from them, placed a vial in front of each of them, and then said, "Take a vial and down all the contents. Understand?"

They both nodded and reached for the vials.

The back door burst open at the exact same time that Indigo lunged toward the twins and screamed, "No!"

Niko used all of his mental energy to break free of Rollins's spell. It took more power than he'd ever used before, but in the chaos, he managed it. The moment he sprung free, he bolted toward the twins and grabbed one of them just before she tilted the potion into her mouth. He grabbed it and threw it across the room, causing the glass to shatter and the potion to spill on the dirty cement floor.

"No!" the twin cried and scrambled for the potion, but it was too late. It was ruined the minute it hit the floor.

Niko turned his attention to Indigo and found she had the other twin by both hands, and her blue ice magic was crawling over the twin's arms. She was reversing the compulsion spell. He wanted to pull Indigo off her. He knew that when she finished reversing the spell, she'd be in no shape to fight off the dean or Paul and his crazy sidekick, Jesse.

But he knew it was too late. She was already in the spell and interrupting her wasn't an option. Instead, he turned to jump back into the fight. And that's when he realized the people who had busted in were none other than Indigo's sisters.

Sage, Lily, and Prim had formed a circle around the dean, Paul, and Jesse and had them locked in a golden magical cage. The amount of magic pouring off them was enough to power an entire state.

Niko took a step back, awed by the power of the sisters. Trusting that they could hold the perpetrators, he moved over to the other twin, who was sitting on the floor, crying over the potion she couldn't take.

"How can I fulfill my duty now?" she asked Niko, her eyes red and tears trickling down her face. "How can I please my creator?"

He was grateful he hadn't eaten much that day, otherwise the contents of his stomach might have ended up on the floor with the spoiled potion. The compulsion spell made these witches see their oppressors as gods. There was nothing more vile than that. "It's going to be okay. I promise. We'll get you what you need in no time."

The twin leaned into him, crying on his shoulder until the other twin ran over and said, "Kimber? Are you okay?

What happened?" she asked Niko and then turned to Indigo. "What's going on?"

"You were compelled," Indigo said softly. "I reversed that spell. Now let me help your sister." Indigo sat down and took Kimber from Niko's arms.

He stared at her, shocked she wasn't passed out on the floor and asked, "How?"

She seemed to understand his question when she nodded to her sisters. "Their power is fueling me."

He made a mental note to send flowers to each of her sisters every week for the next year. After Indigo had freed Kimber of the compulsion spell, he walked the twins out of the back room and into the parking lot, leaving the Easton sisters to keep the dean and his cohorts contained while he called in backup.

The twins clung to each other, both of them pale-faced and confused.

"What happened?" Kinsley asked, her gaze darting from Kimber to Niko. "I don't remember anything."

"I do," Kimber said, her voice wobbly. "Polly told me everything."

That got Niko's attention. He ended his call, confident that a team would be there in moments to contain the dean and company, and then he gave Kimber his full attention. "What do you mean, she told you everything?"

Kimber launched into her story of how Polly also worked at the bar. She found out about the potion operation and was going to turn the dean in, but before she could, they compelled her and forced her to work in their potion factory. Then it burned down and Kimber thought that was the end of it, but they came after Kinsley, and Kimber didn't know why. She started her own investigation into the dean and Paul and learned they had targeted Kinsley to help them get information on Indigo, the creator of the spell.

Kimber turned to her sister. "They were using you to get to Indigo. And once they realized you weren't going to get them what they needed, they compelled you the same way they did Polly. I found out and was so scared. I didn't know what to do. I thought if I could just figure out how to reverse the spell, I could get you out of there and we'd just take off. Get lost somewhere far away from here." She glanced at Niko. "That's why I was at Indigo's office, trying to find notes on the spell. But then she showed up, and the next thing I knew, Officer Pitts was taking me in for questioning. That's all I remember. They must have compelled me, too."

Niko didn't have the heart to tell them that they'd been next on the chopping block. They'd find that out soon enough once charges were filed. For the time being, all they needed to know was that they were safe. "They've been contained," he told them. "This entire operation is over. You're safe now. I promise."

The twins clung to each other as they huddled against the back wall and stayed that way until backup from the MTF arrived. One of the agents took their statements and then indicated to Niko that they'd be treated and offered counseling.

Another team had gone inside and relieved the Easton sisters, and moments later, the dean, Officer Pitts, and Jesse were taken out in magical chains. They wouldn't be going anywhere for a very long time.

All of the Easton sisters looked exhausted when they emerged from the bar's back room. But there was still a sense of absolute power that clung to them.

Niko grinned. "You four could have a place at the MTF if you wanted."

All of them shuddered at once, making him laugh. "I'll take that as a no?"

"It's a definite no," Indigo said. Then she hugged each of her sisters, thanked them, and said, "See you in the morning for coffee?"

"Wouldn't miss it," Sage said.

"Only if there's lemon poppy seed muffins," Lily said.

Prim rolled her eyes. "When isn't there?" The youngest Easton gently squeezed Indigo's hand and said, "See you in the morning, sis." Then she turned to Niko. "Don't keep her up too late. She needs her beauty rest."

They all laughed as the three sisters left together.

"I think I'm in love with the entire Easton family," Niko said.

Indigo just grinned. "Can we go home now?"

"Give me just a minute." He went to talk to the investigating officer in charge, and in a few short moments, he was back by Indigo. "Ready. I told them I'd file my report from home."

"They let you do that?" she asked as he walked her to his truck.

"Sure." He opened the door for her.

She glanced behind her. "What about my SUV?"

"One of the agents will drop it off tonight," he said, tossing one of them her keys. "You don't need to be driving after all that."

She eyed him. "Neither do you."

"Solid point, but I'll have you, so I trust you'll make sure I'm safe," he said with a wink.

"Always. As long as you'll promise to always do the same for me."

"Always," he agreed. Then he leaned in and sealed the deal with a kiss.

There were hoots and hollers from his fellow agents.

Niko just grinned. Then he climbed into his truck and took his girl home.

# CHAPTER 25

## TO WEEKS LATER

P RIM  E ASTON  WALKED  up the pathway to the front door of Gothic Books and grinned at the lights that suddenly came to life in the form of characters from her favorite childhood books. The Velveteen Rabbit hopped away into one of the bushes, while a pants-less bear appeared beside a pink piglet as the two walked into the neighboring woods. A bear in a raincoat bowed to her, while a pig with a spider on its back lay under one of the bushes.

Her sister Indigo had gone all out on spelling the lighting effects for the event. It made her happy to see Indigo fully embracing her magic again. It had been years of her older sister hiding her light under a bushel, and now was her time to shine.

They were all there for the library fundraiser. Prim had done her part by donating a magical quilt. It had been spelled to help its owner's dreams come true. It wasn't a wishing well or anything like that. It was more that it helped nudge the universe in the right direction. She was very proud of it and hoped it went to a good home.

The door swung open all on its own when she stepped up onto the landing.

"Good evening, Ms. Easton," Mateo Silva said as he welcomed her in. "We're pleased you could join us."

She grinned at Dante's stepbrother. He was the manager of the bookstore, and from what she'd heard, everyone in town loved him. And why not? He was both charming and handsome. If he was just five years older, Prim might have already asked him out herself. But alas, not only was she not exactly looking for a date, but she also preferred her men a little less... pretty. Mateo was a little too polished for her.

She chuckled to herself. Look at her, acting as if Mateo Silva was even interested. That was rich. Especially since she hadn't even been asked out since the last disastrous dating incident she'd had three years ago when she'd accidentally spelled her date and he'd ended up with chicken pox on his... well, you know. Let's just say he had a very embarrassing trip to the healer.

That was the kind of thing that stuck to a person.

No one wanted to date the Shlong Pox Girl.

"Prim!" Lily called out, waving for her sister to join her and her partner Braxton. "Over here."

"Is this for me?" Prim asked, taking the champagne glass from her sister's hand and sipping before Lily could even answer.

Brax laughed and handed Lily his glass. "I'll go get another one."

"Make it three!" Lily and Prim called at the same time.

The two sisters looked at each other and cracked up. There had always been an preternatural bond between the two youngest Easton sisters, and this was just one of the ways it manifested.

"Prim, listen," Lily started, but before she could get the words out, Bethany Befana was on the makeshift stage with a microphone in hand.

"Welcome everyone. I want to be the first to thank you for joining us on this momentous occasion. Not only do we have a glorious new bookstore, but the Silvas have brought us much more with the nonprofit library and this venue that they plan to use for all sorts of town events. Give Dante and Mateo a big round of applause!"

The many residents of Befana Bay came through, returning a thunderous applause. When the noise died down, Bethany continued. "As you know, this event is to raise money for the library. The money is to pay the librarian and to further stock the shelves, so don't be shy with your donations. We have a silent auction. You can find the baskets against that back wall. Bidding will continue until 9:00 p.m., so check back often. Don't miss out on something you're dying to have."

There were rumblings among the crowd as they all looked back at the baskets.

Indigo and Niko arrived at that moment, their arms wrapped around each other. Prim stared at them, a little jealous of the obvious affection they had for each other. She didn't relish what they'd had to go through to get together, but she loved seeing her older sister so happy. The pair had been inseparable ever since the takedown of the drug ring a couple of weeks back.

It had been a hectic few days right after all the headlines had come out about the scandal at the school, but in the end, Indigo's reputation had been restored, and there was news that the prosecutor was asking for life imprisonment without parole for the former dean, Officer Pitts, and Jesse. They likely would try to turn on others in their crime organization to reduce their sentences, but most agreed it wouldn't help. Pitts and Rollins were the ringleaders. No one cared as much about those who worked for them.

And with all that mostly behind them, Indigo and Niko were making plans to move in together. Niko was moving to the apartment above the shop so Indigo could stay in Befana Bay, and he'd be renting his house in Hansville to Dante, who had been looking for better accommodations. In the end, everything seemed to be working out for everyone.

Everyone except Prim, who seemed to be in a rut. She'd been doing the same thing day in and day out, working in her fiber shop, going to coven meetings, having lunch with the same people, rarely dating. She was starting to wonder if she needed a shakeup. She just didn't know what that might be.

Her grandmother was still speaking, and Prim tuned in just as she said, "As you know, you were promised a live auction. What you don't know is that it's a bachelorette auction, and first up is Prim Easton!"

Prim stared at her grandmother, her mouth hanging open. "What?" She turned to Indigo. "What did she just say?"

Indigo let out a bark of laughter and then gently pushed her sister toward the stage. "You're up, Prim. Go get that date."

"But—" Prim started.

"Come on," Lily said, grabbing her by the hand and pulling her up on the stage.

There was a smattering of claps, but for the most part the audience was silent.

"You all know my lovely granddaughter, Prim. She runs the fiber store here in town. She's the one to see when you need a fresh ball of cashmere or cotton for that special project."

Still nothing.

"She'll also keep anyone on their toes on a date."

"Isn't that Shlong Pox Girl?" someone called out. Everyone laughed.

"I think it is. Careful guys. Make sure you bring your calamine lotion!" another said.

Bethany cleared her throat and sent the crowd a scathing look. "Everyone in this room has had a spell go bad every now and then. I don't think it's polite to embarrass Prim just because she had a slip of a spell."

There was more laughter, and Prim wanted to die on the spot.

"Can we get this over with?" she whispered to her grandmother, knowing there was no way she'd humiliate herself more by running off the stage.

"Right! Let's start the bidding at one hundred dollars," Bethany called out.

Crickets. You could have heard a pin drop.

Prim swallowed a groan.

"Okay, maybe you just need to warm up. How about seventy-five?"

Silence.

"Fifty?"

Prim stared at her feet, wishing a lightning bolt would come down and strike her dead rather than suffer this humiliation.

"Twenty-five dollars?" Bethany asked with a bit of desperation in her tone.

"One thousand dollars," a man called out.

Everyone turned to see who it was, and then they parted ways as Dante Silva walked up to the stage and held his hand out to Prim.

"Sold! One thousand dollars to the gorgeous Dante Silva," Bethany called into the mic.

Prim stared at Dante, her mouth hanging open.

"Take his hand, Prim," Lily hissed from behind her.

"Right." Prim slipped her hand into Dante's and let him help her off the stage.

They walked through the crowd and headed to the small patio out back where they had some privacy.

"Thank you, Dante," Prim said in a rush. "But really, you didn't have to do that. It's too much, I—"

Dante held up two fingers, silencing her, and then said, "I didn't do it for you. I did it for me."

Before she could say another word, he walked off, leaving her on the patio completely dumbfounded.

# DEANNA'S BOOK LIST

**<u>Witches of Keating Hollow:</u>**
Soul of the Witch
Heart of the Witch
Spirit of the Witch
Dreams of the Witch
Courage of the Witch
Love of the Witch
Power of the Witch
Essence of the Witch
Muse of the Witch
Vision of the Witch
Waking of the Witch
Honor of the Witch
Promise of the Witch
Return of the Witch
Fortune of the Witch
Song of the Witch

Rise of the Witch

**Keating Hollow Happily Ever Afters:**
Gift of the Witch
Wisdom of the Witch
Light of the Witch

**Witches of Befana Bay:**
The Witch's Silver Lining
The Witch's Secret Love
The Witch's Lost Spell
The Witch's Hidden Garden

**Witches of Christmas Grove:**
A Witch For Mr. Holiday
A Witch For Mr. Christmas
A Witch For Mr. Winter
A Witch For Mr. Mistletoe
A Witch For Mr. Frost
A Witch For Mr. Garland
A Witch For Mr. Bell

**Premonition Pointe Novels:**
Witching For Grace
Witching For Hope
Witching For Joy
Witching For Clarity
Witching For Moxie
Witching For Kismet

## Miss Matched Midlife Dating Agency:
Star-crossed Witch
Honor-bound Witch
Outmatched Witch
Moonstruck Witch
Rainmaker Witch

## Jade Calhoun Novels:
Haunted on Bourbon Street
Witches of Bourbon Street
Demons of Bourbon Street
Angels of Bourbon Street
Shadows of Bourbon Street
Incubus of Bourbon Street
Bewitched on Bourbon Street
Hexed on Bourbon Street
Dragons of Bourbon Street

## Pyper Rayne Novels:
Spirits, Stilettos, and a Silver Bustier
Spirits, Rock Stars, and a Midnight Chocolate Bar
Spirits, Beignets, and a Bayou Biker Gang
Spirits, Diamonds, and a Drive-thru Daiquiri Stand
Spirits, Spells, and Wedding Bells

## Ida May Chronicles:
Witched To Death
Witch, Please
Stop Your Witchin'

## Crescent City Fae Novels:
Influential Magic
Irresistible Magic
Intoxicating Magic

## Last Witch Standing:
Bewitched by Moonlight
Soulless at Sunset
Bloodlust By Midnight
Bitten At Daybreak

## Witch Island Brides:
The Wolf's New Year Bride
The Vampire's Last Dance
The Warlock's Enchanted Kiss
The Shifter's First Bite

## Destiny Novels:
Defining Destiny
Accepting Fate

## Wolves of the Rising Sun:
Jace
Aiden
Luc
Craved
Silas
Darien
Wren

## Black Bear Outlaws:
Cyrus

Chase

Cole

## Bayou Springs Alien Mail Order Brides:
Zeke

Gunn

Echo

# ABOUT THE AUTHOR

New York Times and USA Today bestselling author, Deanna Chase, is a native Californian, who now splits her time between New Orleans and the Pacific Northwest. When she isn't writing, she is often goofing off with her husband, traveling, or playing with her two dogs. For more information and updates on newest releases visit her website at deannachase.com.

www.ingramcontent.com/pod-product-compliance
Lightning Source LLC
Chambersburg PA
CBHW020059180626
46812CB00006B/2391